Venomous DECEIT

USA TODAY BESTSELLING AUTHOR

T.L. SMITH

Venomous Deceit

Copyright @ T.L. Smith Books PTY LTD 2026

All Rights Reserved

This book is a work of fiction. Any references to real events, real people, and real places are used fictitiously. Other names, characters, places, and incidents are products of the Author's imagination and any resemblance to persons, living or dead, actual events, organizations or places is entirely coincidental. All rights are reserved. This book is intended for the purchaser of this book ONLY. No part of this book may be reproduced or transmitted in any form or by any means, graphic, electronic, or mechanical, including photocopying, recording, taping, or by any information storage retrieval system, without the express written permission of the Author. All songs, song titles and lyrics contained in this book are the property of the respective songwriters and copyright holders.

CAUTION

I'm not to blame when you dig for dirt on me... and end up wanting me to bury you in something else entirely.

I was supposed to expose him.
Soren Nixon, the untouchable media mogul, the one
who hides behind locked doors and whispered oaths.
My job was simple.
Uncover the truth behind The Forsaken Society.
But nothing about him is simple.
I found a man who is carved from control and sin,
who spends his free time fighting in underground
rings to feel something real.
He's dangerous in ways I can't write about,
intoxicating in ways I can't resist.
Every secret pulls me deeper into his world.
Every touch makes me forget my purpose.
He's everything I should fear.
But when he looks at me as if I am already his, I start
to wonder. Maybe the story I have been chasing is
the one that will destroy me.

ONE

CRESSIDA

Case Notes

Assess how he is in a place that is not work.

PEOPLE ARE SWEATY. Loud. Drunk. Disgusting, really. The air reeks of spilled beer and desperation as voices clash over who will win. Pushing through the crowd, I bump shoulders with a lot of men, even some women dressed in barely-there clothes as they scream at the two men fighting in the ring.

Something lands on my cheek, and I wipe it away, realizing it's more than likely someone's spit, and I instantly recoil in disgust. The air is muggy from so many people crammed together in such a tight space. The closer I get to the ring, the stronger the metallic scent of blood and stale alcohol becomes, mingling with the unmistakable tang of sex.

Clutching my phone in one hand and my keys in the other, I continue walking until I reach the center, which is roped off. I'm actually amazed that no one steps over it, as it's not much of a barrier. One man, clearly knocked out and not able to walk, is being dragged away by two other men while the announcer, a woman dressed in leather, steps into the middle of the makeshift ring. She looks like she could be one of the wrestlers on television, the perfect mix of bulky and beautiful.

"Now, we all know our next fighter is a regular here," she begins. "But his opponent is someone new, someone exciting. He's been known to win a fight or two, and we are excited to have him."

Everyone starts clapping, and I watch as people shift to make room for the two men who walk out toward either side of the ring. Loud cheers echo through the room as the newcomer, dressed only in boxing shorts and his hands wrapped with some type of material, steps into the ring. And then the cheers grow louder as the reason I'm here tonight comes into view. Soren Nixon. Screams erupt, more deafening than for his opponent.

I try to push closer to the front, only managing a spot just behind a couple with a ringside view. The woman looks over her shoulder at me, eyes me up and down, and with a raised brow, she asks, "You in the wrong place?"

I look down at my pants, which are part of a suit. I'd taken the jacket off to blend in, but clearly, I did a terrible job. I'd popped a few of the buttons on my white shirt to tease a little bit of cleavage, but that apparently hasn't helped, and sweat is pooling between my breasts in the thick heat.

"I'm fucking the fighter," I reply with a smile, hoping she won't ask me anything more.

"Yeah, you and every other girl in here wishes." She laughs as the man with her says something in her ear, to which she shrugs, then redirects her attention back to the two fighters.

I watch Soren bounce from one foot to the other. My eyes can't help but scan over his thick arms, corded with muscles. His hair is a mess, but somehow fits him perfectly. He's lethal-looking up there; there's no point denying that. All I have to do is glance around the room—women and men all stare at him, their gazes hungry and riveted on him. He's basically sin, wrapped in danger, cloaked in an enigma, and nothing fascinates me more than uncovering people's secrets, and his I'm very interested in. I've been trying to get dirt on him for over a year, and other than the knowledge that he's a part of some secret society, I don't have much else. I've heard a lot of gossip and rumors, but I have no hard facts. It seems that if anyone talks, they disappear. And when I mentioned the words "the hunt" to him, his face constricted, and I knew he wanted me gone, like I had just touched on something I should not have. His silence says more than words ever could.

It's not that easy to deter me, though.

I'm determined to find out *all* his secrets.

Hence, why I'm here.

The crowd starts chanting his name, but he doesn't seem to care. You can clearly see which fighters are here for the fame and which for the rush. Soren is all about the rush. He doesn't glance into the crowd, doesn't need the validation, while the other fighter can't stop searching faces for approval. Soren has already gone somewhere else—locked in, waiting for the moment when blood and adrenaline will take over.

Someone rings a bell, and before another word is spoken, the two fighters move.

Soren glides along the floor as the other guy steps up to him, fists raised. He swings, and Soren ducks effortlessly. The other guy keeps throwing punches as the crowd chants Soren's name and shouts for him to "end him." The fight has barely started, but the other fighter is already missing his mark, growing sloppy and winded with every swing.

He grunts something at Soren that makes Soren tense before the guy swings at him, this time landing the blow. But Soren reacts quickly. He steps back and shakes it off before advancing on the other fighter, who's smirking now because he finally got a hit in. Soren jabs him in the face, not once, not twice, but three times consecutively. And the other fighter falls straight onto his ass, the crowd cheering loudly.

"Knockout."

It's chanted over and over again.

Soren goes to leave the ring while the other guy struggles and fails to sit up. The woman in front of me screams Soren's name, making him pause. His eyes flick in our direction before drifting across the room, sharp and searching.

Just when I think he's about to leave, his attention shifts back in our direction, and his stormy gray eyes land directly on me. His lip curls up in disgust before he starts walking my way. I stay where I am, unable to move even if I wanted to. Having a man as powerful as he is stalking toward you after he just knocked someone out is somewhat intimidating, to say the least. I note a thin drip of blood on his lip as he climbs over the rope and pushes through until he's standing right in front of me. The air between us thickens, heavy with adrenaline and something else I can't quite name, and it feels like everything falls silent before his lips start to move.

"What are you doing here?" he hisses at me, his voice low, rough, smoky and spent—like someone who just finished fucking and lit a cigarette. He's barely keeping his anger in check as his eyes narrow on me, and I blink to escape the trance his voice puts me in.

"I—" His demeanour makes me lose my words.

"She said she was fucking a fighter," the woman from earlier shouts above the din of the crowd.

His gray gaze flicks to her, then comes back to me. "Fucking a fighter?" he asks, his lips quirking in amusement. *Asshole.*

"I was just leaving." I jerk my thumb over my shoulder.

He steps up extremely close, then leans down

and gets in my face. "No, you aren't. You've been following me for way too long, Miss Knight."

"So, you've done your research," I say sarcastically, resisting the urge to rest my hand on my hip, while trying to swallow down nerves that are bubbling up with his closeness.

"Oh, have I ever." Soren dips his head even closer, his nose skimming past my cheek, his mouth gazing far too close to my ear. "Tell me, who is with your son right now?"

I gasp, my stomach pitching, but it's fury at his question and the veiled threat behind it that tightens my fists at my sides. In that moment, the people around us fade into nothing, the noise dulling until it's just him and me. This man has done his digging, and he's done it well.

I don't post my son on social media at all because I try to keep him out of the public eye as much as possible. Not just because I investigate some weird things in my job, but also because his father has requested it. I'm on good terms with Oliver's father, and I want to keep it that way. Even though our relationship didn't work out, he is a good father.

"How dare you?" I seethe, stepping closer, until I can smell the sweat covering his body.

"*Me?* How dare *I?*" He laughs, slowly and mean,

as if he already knows how this ends. "Have you forgotten you take every opportunity to follow me and dig into *my* business?" he reminds me.

"It's my job. I go where the story is. And *you* have a story, Soren."

Someone bumps me from behind, and it pushes me straight into his arms. He grabs me, one hand on my arm, the other settling on my waist, warm and... *possessive?* He doesn't push me away. He holds me there, like he's deciding what to do next.

"And it's my job to make sure I'm not being stalked by crazy women who want what I have." I'm acutely aware of his touch right now.

"Believe me, you have nothing *I* want."

"Oh, really?" He bends down, and his face is so close to mine that for a moment I think he'll kiss me. Instead, he shakes his head, huffing out a breath. "So, why do you keep stalking me?"

"Stalk? That's a word you clearly don't know the true definition. I attend places where you happen to be, for work," I explain.

I'm jostled again as the crowd starts to move, and my hands fall to his hard chest. Glancing down at the spot where my skin touches his, I quickly pull them away because his chest is hot to touch. As I do, he releases me, and I turn away to leave, but his hand shoots out and grips my wrist, his fingers wrapped tightly.

"This is not the end of this discussion." He tries to say more, but we're shoved again. With an exasperated huff, he grabs hold of me, lifts me like I weigh nothing, and tosses me over his shoulder. I let out a startled cry as the room spins, his shoulder digging into my stomach. Then he strides straight through the crowd, carrying me like I'm his to take, like possession is the language he speaks fluently, and I'm struggling to translate it.

"Put. Me. Down! What the *hell* are you even doing?" I scream.

He bounces me—yes, bounces me—on his shoulder, pressing further into my stomach as he strides to an exit that I'm guessing leads to the changing room. Once the door shuts behind us, he sets me down on my feet, then turns to open a locker and pulls out his belongings.

There's a shower to his right, and without a second thought, he removes his shorts and then walks over and turns it on. All I can do is stare at his rock-hard ass. I'm completely confused as to what is going on and why he dragged me back here. *Who gave him the right to put his hands on me like that?* I go to speak, but my words are completely cut off when he turns around with absolutely no shame whatsoever and starts washing his body.

"So, you do know how to shut up," he says, then proceeds to wash his cock right there in front of me. "Risky for you to come in here dressed like that. You do know this place is full of criminals." His gaze rakes over me while he finishes cleaning his cock. He tilts his head back, and the water streams over his skin, removing all the soap. I watch in complete fascination as the suds slip all the way down, past his cock to his feet, and then scuttle down the drain.

He has the nicest body I've ever seen, all raw strength and sculpted muscle. Every ridge and line looks carved with precision, his abs taut, his chest broad, his arms thick with the kind of power that only comes from years of discipline, not vanity. My ex-husband, Noah, was fit—gym-fit, predictable-fit, the kind that came from routine and protein shakes. But he wasn't this type of fit. Soren is built for endurance, for impact. Every inch of him radiates controlled aggression and effortless dominance. He's a walking embodiment of danger wrapped in temptation with a pretty little bow on top.

"What's wrong with what I'm wearing?" I ask, even though I know perfectly well now that it's the wrong choice for a place like this.

"Nothing, if you're in a damn office." He turns off the water, then walks straight up to me.

"Your cock is pointing in my direction," I say, and he smirks.

"You're in *my domain*, Miss Knight. If at any time my cock offends you, you could leave instead of just standing there, staring at it."

He does have a mighty fine cock—thick, impressive, and easily the largest I have ever seen.

"You manhandled me," I growl, heat rising in my voice.

"I saved you from getting trampled by the crowd. A thank you will suffice."

He hasn't made any move to get dressed, standing there completely unfazed and confident in his own skin, as if the very idea of modesty does not apply to him.

"No, I don't think so."

He nods, as if he were expecting that answer. He gets closer, and I brace myself, for him. But he simply leans around me, his body pressing slightly against mine as he opens what I assume is his locker, and produces a towel. He says nothing, and neither do I as I turn away from him and he slides on his pants.

But I stare.

I can't help it.

Because damn.

Every muscle in his back flexes as he moves, and I swear my common sense packs up and leaves.

Because even though I know I shouldn't be back here, I can't seem to make my feet move.

TWO

SOREN

SHE MAKES no attempt to leave, though I can see in her eyes that she is itching to run.

Reaching back into my locker, I grab my shirt. Without bothering to put it on, I shut the locker with a solid clang, and turn to face her. She looks so prim and proper, so out of place here. My eyes skim over her tailored pants and tight shirt with just a touch of cleavage peeking out. Her face is flawless, and without a lick of makeup to be seen, so different from the usual women I keep in my company. She has a flicker of defiance and curiosity that glosses over her face. She is not afraid, not really. Just smart enough to know she should be.

"Let's go." I nod toward the door.

"I have a few questions to ask you," she says. I shake my head and start walking, her heels clicking behind me as she follows.

"You already know my answer," I reply.

She huffs out a breath of annoyance. "*No comment,*" she grumbles, giving me the answer I tell her over and over again. "Just this once. Come on, give me *something.*" I hold the door open for her, and she stops halfway out to look back at me. "You should know I won't stop until I get a story."

"And you should know I will *never* talk." I smile at her, the cold air hitting my bare chest.

"So, you admit there is *something* to talk about?" One of her perfect brows rises at my answer.

"Where is your car?" I ask. It's late, and the people who come to these events aren't always here just for the thrill. Some come because they're as fucked-up as I am. Predators in the dark, looking for an outlet, a target, or someone to bleed with. This woman doesn't belong here, and that's a problem I can't ignore.

"Why?"

"Because it's time for you to go home. Now, where is it?"

She turns and points to a little red car. I usher

her toward it, and when we reach it, she gets out her keys and opens the door.

"Goodnight, Cressida. I hope I *never* see you here again."

She rolls her eyes, and I want to spank her for her attitude. But instead, I clench my teeth as she bends ever so slightly to throw her bag onto the passenger seat, and I can't help but look down at her ass. Glancing over her shoulder, she catches me but doesn't say a word regarding my lingering stare.

"Oh, you'll see me again. I can't resist seeing that handsome face." She offers me a full, white-toothed smile before she gets into her car. I stand, unmoving, as she shuts the door and then starts the car. And I wonder why I haven't discarded her yet. I have done so to many people for less—yet, here she is, still breathing. I watch her drive off until her taillights disappear, then I head to my own car.

I drove my Porsche here last time, only to come out and find it stolen. Now I drive a much less conspicuous car. As I get into my Toyota, my phone rings before I can even start the engine. Glancing down at it, I see my sister's name flash on the screen.

I love my sister. *A lot.* She has health issues, and we don't have any other family, so I've taken care of her all my adult life. And sometimes, just sometimes, it's tiring as fuck. Contemplating not answering it, I sit and let it ring a few times. Then I finally accept the call and put the phone to my ear.

"Maya, it's late" are the first words I say to her.

Maya and I are close, but there are many things I don't share with her. She knows about the Forsaken Society, sure, but not everything that comes with it—the secrets, the deals, and the darkness that hides behind the masks. She has been to parties, brushed shoulders with the members, and for a while, she thought she could handle it. She even asked me to pair her with one of them.

I did.

Big mistake.

It went to fucking shit faster than either of us saw coming.

"I know. I just wanted to know if I can borrow the jet."

"What?" I say, shaking my head.

"I want to go to Las Vegas."

"Goodnight." I hang up on her.

Maya needs to get a damn job and stop living off my money. She's a grown-ass woman, but anytime I mention her working, she uses her illness to tug on my heartstrings. She has a weak heart, and while it was touch-and-go for a bit, lately she's been healthy. So, I'm hoping, even though she's annoying some-times, that it stays that way. I adore my sister, but at times I wish she would live her own life, instead of intruding on mine.

THREE
CRESSIDA

My job is to investigate things that the everyday person could never even fathom. I interview some of the worst people who have ever lived. And I love it. I understand this job isn't for everyone—it's fucked-up, some of the stuff I uncover. It also makes me extremely paranoid and even more protective of my son.

I went to college for journalism, but working for a local newspaper is worlds apart from being in the chaos of a big media corporation. Thankfully, my ex was well-connected, and when I first started out, he pulled some strings to get me an internship at one of the big digital news outlets. I clawed my way up from there, one late-night deadline at a time. A few years later, they gave me my first big lead, and I have been addicted to the chase ever since. And it's what I love.

A lot of my stories go viral, which keeps me comfortably paid. My boss wants to keep his golden goose happy and on his staff.

I was at a work event when I first saw Soren. He's pretty well known in media circles. He owns and operates a large corporation and is the media mogul of many news channels. Not the one I work for, which I think he hates because no matter how much he tries to stop me, it won't work.

"Soren called." I lift my head to find my boss, Michael, at my office door as I'm packing up to leave for the day.

"And?" I pull my bag strap over my shoulder. The damn thing is heavy, with my laptop weighing it down.

"He said you've been harassing him."

"There's a big story there. Do you *not* want to be the first to drop it?" I ask.

"You weren't meant to go after him. We have discussed this. Soren is powerful. I want you to remember that." Michael isn't telling me to stop, but his warning is clear. He understands what I'm doing, even if he disagrees with it.

"I get it, and I'll be careful." I smile at him. I

didn't tell him about going to the fight last night because I don't have to share the details of my investigation with him. I only have to show him the outcome of my research, which works well for both of us because he doesn't have to lecture me about how I shouldn't be doing certain things, and I don't have to listen to the lecture and then ignore whatever he's said. I like to investigate stories on my own because I feel like I have a more personal connection when I do it myself.

I catch the train back to my place. Noah is already inside with Oliver when I open the door. We both have a key to each other's homes. Though we're no longer together, we're still good friends. We understand that we don't use the keys unless it involves our son, and the other person has to approve it first.

"Mom, you're home." Oliver, who is seven, looks up from where he and Noah sit with a pizza between them on the kitchen table.

"I see you cooked." I waggle my brows at them.

"I got in late... pizza was the easiest choice," Noah says, then stands. He wipes his hands on his blue trousers. He looks good, though he never really looks bad.

"Got a hot date tonight?" I ask him as I walk over

and kiss his cheek. He kisses mine back and then shakes his head.

"No, just working late."

Noah's a banker, and he's a good one. His family owns a lot of commercial property, so he's always been well off. I come from a more modest background, but we didn't do badly for ourselves either. Still, I wouldn't be where I am today without his help or the influence of his family.

"Can I chat with you outside?" Noah asks and nods toward the door. I kiss Oliver's head as I put my bag down, then I follow Noah out. I shut the door so our voices won't carry back to Oliver.

"I had a visitor today," he tells me, sliding his hands into his pockets.

"Okay," I reply, confused as to what that has to do with me.

"Soren Nixon was waiting outside my building today when I left to pick up Oliver." I bite my lip at that information. Of course, he was. "He mentioned he knows you."

"He doesn't know me," I bite back, harder than I intended.

Noah lifts his hand and runs it through his blond hair. "Okay. Well, I just wanted to say, if you're doing a story on him—"

"What?"

"If you are, just be careful."

"Do you think I'm ever *not* careful?" I place my hand on my hip and scowl.

"I know you are an independent woman and don't need a man's help. But, Cressida, I still care about you and never want anything to happen to you."

"Thanks, but I'll be fine. I always am." I smile, and he gives me a disbelieving look in return. I don't mention the small threat that Soren made because I'm always careful when it comes to Oliver, but I can't lie and say it didn't shake me up a little bit.

Our marriage was over years before we got divorced. We knew it was never going to work, but we tried to stay together for Oliver. Doing the right thing for our son is the one thing we will always agree on.

We change the subject, and he tells me about Oliver's day before he says he has to go. I stand on the stoop, watching him leave for a few minutes before I finally head inside.

I've been single for two years now, and I haven't really moved on. A part of me is scared to because I don't want to bring strange men around my son. He already has a great father, so I don't want or need someone stepping in when it's not necessary.

When I step back into the kitchen, I find Oliver already cleaning up after dinner. He's a perfect mix of Noah and me. He has Noah's eyes but my almost-black hair. He also has the kind of smile that makes my heart happy whenever I see him. If I'm having a bad day, I picture his bright grin, and it instantly improves.

I approach and wrap my arms around his small body. He's getting bigger and bigger every day, it seems. I can't get over the fact that I'm raising a little man, and he's going to be amazing. He has excellent manners and does well in school. I didn't realize how lucky I could be until I had him.

While Oliver is used to being around Noah's side of the family, he's not as familiar with my side. We try to make it out to see my family at least once a year, but we haven't visited them in more than a year because I've been so busy with work, and they live on the other side of the country and hate flying.

Noah's family spoils Oliver because he's their only grandson. Noah is the oldest of his siblings and was the first to have a child. It doesn't help that he is also the favorite among his side of the family. I wouldn't be surprised if they leave everything to

Oliver. He does no wrong in their eyes, and a part of me loves that. Loves that he has a connection with people who are always going to have his back. A lot of people in this world don't get that luxury.

"I missed you today, buddy." I hold him a little tighter.

"I missed you too," he says with a squeeze that is almost too big for his little arms.

"How was school?"

"Good. I got an A in math. Dad thinks I'll be an amazing banker." He laughs.

"Only if that's what you want," I tell him, knowing he's always wanted to be a banker like his father.

"My teacher asked me how you are."

I lean back and look down at him. "What do you mean?"

"He said he loves your writing and is sad he hasn't seen anything from you in a while."

I smile as I brush Oliver's hair away from his face.

"Tell him I'm working on something big," I reply, then kiss his cheek. "Now, bedtime."

"Can I play *Fortnite*?" he begs.

"No. You know you're only allowed to play that game on the weekends." I shake my head at him.

"Okay," he says, but it is tinged with disappointment.

I watch as he sulks off up the stairs to his room, then I check my phone and see an email from a name I know well.

Good afternoon, Miss Knight,
I have concluded that you won't stop harassing me until you get what you want.
So, I will give you the interview you have been requesting.
Under one condition...
From,
The Man You Stalk

THE MAN I STALK. I let out a little laugh.

Well, I guess it's partially true.

FOUR
SOREN

Once she reads the email, I get a notification and wait for her to reply. When I don't get a response after ten minutes, I turn off my phone and step into the shower. She's been investigating me, but I've been doing some digging of my own. I can easily do this with the help of my fellow Society member, Boston, who is a detective and will get me anything I ask for. But I feel like with her, I can tend to it myself, except she doesn't seem intimidated by me. Actually, she seems to think she is in control, which is amusing in itself.

I keep a lot of pieces of my life hidden, and I'm good at it. Otherwise, I wouldn't be the Lord of the Forsaken Society. I'm a natural-born leader, and I don't take my position lightly, but I do revel in being in charge. And while the Forsaken doesn't take up all my time, it does take up a good chunk of it, especially when it involves the hunt. The hunt is held twice a year, and I select the chosen prey. Usually, Boston finds fucked-up people, and we choose from them, but sometimes someone will piss me off so much that I'll be vindictive enough to pick them as our quarry. It doesn't happen often, but when it does, no one else knows apart from me—that is, until the hunt is over.

It's one of the perks of being in charge.

The time for another hunt is upon us, and I've been so preoccupied I haven't had a chance to look at the options Boston sent me. So, after I shower, I sit on my brown leather couch, wrapped in just a towel, and check the files.

The first option is a man known to kill women while they're walking alone to their cars late at night. Boston hasn't caught him yet because he's good at hiding, but he knows who the man is. A picture in the file shows he's a large man, which means he would probably be caught easily and too quickly, so he goes into the reject pile. We want them to run and lead us on a long and exciting chase. It's the chase we crave.

My phone alerts me to an incoming email just as

I pick up another file. Reaching for it, I see Cressida's name on the screen.

> *Hello, Soren.*
>
> *I appreciate very much that you have granted me an interview. What is your one condition?*
>
> *Please let me know at your earliest convenience.*
>
> *From,*
> *Your Stalker*

I CAN'T HELP but smirk at her response.

Sitting back, I type a reply.

> *Miss Knight,*
>
> *Thank you for your prompt response. It's appreciated.*
>
> *The one condition is that you accompany me to an event first, this time with an invite, since we both know how you like to sneak into them.*

From,

The Man You Stalk

P.S. Thanks for admitting that you are
a stalker.

CRESSIDA HAS a way of getting into events without being invited. It's probably one of the reasons she's so good at her job. She's even managed to get into one of the Forsaken's wive's parties, which is an event where wives are only invited, which is different to the girlfriend parties where members bring a woman and are free to share her if that's what they wish. And a lot of them do.

There are only three members who don't do that —myself, Reon, and Arlo. The idea of sharing doesn't appeal to me. Reon isn't the type to share, even more so now that he's happily married and in love with his wife. And Arlo hasn't taken part in the sharing at the girlfriend parties since before he met Cora.

We established a rule a long time ago that states if you aren't married by the age of thirty, the Society will honorably assist you in finding a wife. Though I am well past thirty now, I remain unmarried and have no plans to change that anytime soon. Maybe someday I'll do it just so I'm following rules set in motion by me, or perhaps I won't. One of the perks of being the Lord is that I can get away with skirting the rules, unlike a regular member.

Members of the Forsaken come from various backgrounds—some are from prominent families, some have valuable connections, but most have a lot of money and fucked-up tendencies.

I am the Lord because I am Forsaken royalty. My great-grandfather was a Lord. After him, leadership passed to someone who wasn't blood-related, but eventually it came back to me, where it will stay until I die.

FIVE
CRESSIDA

Case Notes

*I guess this one I don't have to sneak
into.*

He wants me to go to an event. It takes me a day to
form a reply, and I read it several times before sending it.

*Good afternoon, Soren,
I apologize for the delay in responding;
work has been busy.*

I would be happy to accompany you to an event in exchange for your story.
Thank you again.
No longer your stalker thanks to your invite.

I'VE SNUCK into several parties, and now he's inviting me to one. There has to be some catch to this. He would never willingly take me to an event, especially knowing how hard I've been digging into him.

Less than two minutes after I sent the message to Soren, I receive a response. I power down my work laptop, grab my coat and bag, and head out.

Answer your phone.

THEN MY PHONE RINGS, the call coming from a private number. I get a lot of calls from private numbers, tips, and similar information for stories from people who wish to remain anonymous.

Pressing accept, I hear his low and smoky voice echo through the phone, sending shivers racing all over my body when he says my name.

"Cressida Knight."

"Soren Nixon."

"Are you ready?" he asks.

"Ready?" I question, confused as I hail a cab in front of my office building. When one pulls up, I climb in and cover the mic, I rattle off my address before I turn my attention back to Soren. "Ready for what?"

"I'm standing outside your house. Are you ready?"

"A-Are you joking?" I stammer as the driver navigates through the traffic.

"Do you think I'm the type of man who jokes, Miss Knight?"

"Well, no, but who doesn't give a woman notice before showing up at her door and expecting her to be ready to go somewhere when she didn't even know the date and time?"

"I'm giving you notice right now as I stand here waiting for you." Then he hangs up on me.

For fuck's sake.

What an asshole!

Noting where we are, I realize we're still more

than ten minutes away from my house, and that's if the traffic cooperates. My leg bounces anxiously as I stare out the window, watching the city blur past in streaks of light and motion, silently urging the driver to go faster. The hum of the engine and the flicker of passing traffic do nothing to calm the storm twisting in my stomach.

The traffic isn't too bad, and when we reach my street, my pulse spikes. He's there. Leaning against the building in his pristine suit, head bent toward his phone. When his gray eyes lift and lock on me as I push open the cab door, the rest of the world seems to fade away. His gaze rakes over me, slowly and deliberately, and I swear the air thickens between us.

I know I'm not dressed for whatever function he wants me to go to, but if he's giving me no time to change into something more appropriate, he's going to have to accept me as I am. Thankfully, Oliver is with Noah tonight, so I don't have to explain the man waiting for me.

"Ready?" I ask, and I can feel my cheeks heat from the look he gives me.

"If you are," he replies, and that's when I notice his driver waiting for us.

Soren walks over to the car and holds the door open for me. I race to my house door, unlock it, put my laptop bag inside, then relock the door and run to the car, where he's still waiting by the back door.

As I slide into the car, I feel his gaze locked on me. I'm dressed in black pants with a designer belt around my waist, and my shirt is baby blue. It's tight-fitting. Definitely not an outfit to wear to anything fancier than a work event, and this man looks like he's going to a gala.

The car ride passes mostly in silence, and Soren ignores me for the majority of the drive. I'm unsure what to say. He hasn't technically given me the go-ahead for the interview yet, and I don't want to over-step because I *really* want to interview him. It would be detrimental to my job if I missed out on this opportunity.

"Where is the event?" I ask.

He looks up from his phone, and the light hits his high cheekbones as he stares at me with stormy eyes.

"We're almost there," he tells me in a bored tone, his gaze lingering on me.

I'm the first to look away, and I glance out the window to see where we are. This place is known for hosting the fanciest galas, and here I am, with a man dressed like a fucking God while I'm wearing my dowdy work clothes.

The car door is opened for me when we come to

a stop, and when I step out, the valet gives me a look, confused by my outfit, but then quickly covers his reaction.

Yeah, thanks for that. If I didn't already feel inadequate, I definitely do now.

I see a few people I recognize entering the venue, and I assume they are members of the Society. A few of them give Soren a simple head nod as he steps up next to me.

"Do you just plan to stand there?" he asks.

"Do you plan to guide me in?"

His glare traces over my body before he says, "Dressed like that? No." And then he walks away.

My mouth falls open in shock, and I wonder if it's too late to turn around and go home.

But I *need* the fucking story.

I *want* the fucking story.

And the bastard knows that.

So, I follow him up the stairs, where the door is opened for him as if he's the man of the hour. He doesn't thank the person who opened it. In fact, he doesn't even make eye contact with them.

Asshole.

The moment we step inside, I know it's a black-tie event, and I am clearly not dressed for this at all. I hear a few announcements from the stage and realize this is an awards ceremony.

What the actual fuck?

Rushing my steps, I get in line with him and hiss, "Is this some type of award show?"

He looks down at me, as if I'm less than him, and lacking in some way.

"It's a recognition gala." He waits for me to say something else, but I can't. He's brought me to an event that I've never been invited to, but have heard of. It's a night when major publishers, news agencies, and other media outlets receive awards for their achievements.

"The star of the show is here," someone says from behind us. I turn to see a woman in a stunning red dress that almost matches the red carpet, except her dress is sparkly. She offers her hand to Soren with a smile, and he takes it and leans down to kiss the top of her hand.

I scoff, louder than I anticipated. Soren's standard settings include rudeness and bluntness, so this must all be an act on his part right now.

"It's so good to see you, Soren. I feel like it's been way too long. Tell me, when are you going to accept that invitation I keep extending?" She gushes a little too hard before he releases her hand. She immediately takes that same hand and places it on his chest. She doesn't pick up on the way he tenses at her touch—he's obviously uncomfortable with it. But he is being polite, which makes me want to laugh. He takes a half step back, just enough that she's no longer touching him.

"I'm sorry, Miranda. As you can imagine, I've been swamped. Please, let me introduce you to my girlfriend." He waves toward me, and I stare at him in utter shock.

Did he really *just say that and look directly at me?*

Miranda eyes me cautiously, but also with a look of hurt etched on her face. She wasn't expecting that response, but then again, neither was I.

"This is Cressida. She came here straight after work to support me, so you'll have to excuse her attire." His gaze sweeps over me briefly before it fixes back on her. And all I can do is stand here in stunned silence while being judged.

Should I correct him? It's risky because he could end our agreement at any time. I will do a lot of things to get a story, apparently even pretend to be the girlfriend of an obnoxious jerk. Go figure!

"Oh, that explains your lack of formal wear. I

was surprised they let you in. Maybe they thought you were one of the workers." She laughs.

"So what if I were?" I question with a fake smile etched on my face.

She waves a dismissive hand at me. Then, without a care that his "girlfriend" is standing right next to him, she touches him again in a more-than-friendly manner. I notice his subtle flinch, and it's so clear he doesn't want her touch any more than I want to be here.

He once again shifts away from beneath her hand, and she brings it up to rest on her chest, where the swell of her breasts presses against the neckline of her top, a deliberate display of soft skin framed by the low dip of fabric meant to draw attention. I know she's waiting for his gaze to drop, for that flicker of male interest she's used to commanding. But it doesn't happen. His eyes stay on her face, unbothered, and, unreadable. Then slowly, he scans the room, his gaze skimming over me before settling back on her.

"You must excuse us; I'm needed."

Without even glancing back, he reaches for me, his hand finding mine easily. His palm is so much larger than mine, and his grip is firm and unyielding. I try to pull away, but it's useless as he leads me away from Miranda. I go because, really, what else am I supposed to do? Under normal circumstances, I'd kick him or tell him exactly where to shove it, but this isn't normal. I'm standing in a room full of prominent people in my field whom I want to impress, and every one of them is watching.

So, I let him drag me over to someone I recognize but don't really know personally—Arlo Graves. A highly respected therapist. Probably one of the most sought-after among the extremely wealthy.

"I see you brought company. Did you not tell her about the dress code?" Arlo drawls.

Soren spares me a look, and I know he can see the flush of embarrassment on my cheeks as I once again try to pull my hand from his.

"Cressida, is that you?" I turn my head to watch Cora approaching in a stunning light-pink dress and bright-pink heels. "It's been too long. How is work?"

Soren stares at me, waiting for me to speak.

"Good" is all I can give her in reply.

"Are you crashing the party?" Cora asks.

The last time I crashed one of the parties, I used Arlo's interest in her as my way in. Now they're together and clearly happy, as evidenced by her bright smile while his hand skates around her waist, and he pulls her against his side.

I've warned her about their reputations and that of the Forsaken. About how people have mysteriously gone missing. And while no evidence points to them, I know their secret little Society has something to do with it.

"You could say I was dragged here." I smile and lift the hand that is still clasped in Soren's.

SIX

SOREN

THE REASON I invited Cressida is that I needed a buffer from Miranda. The woman has been messaging me all week, telling me how excited she is to see me again. I've never given Miranda *any* indication that I'm interested in her, even though she's thrown up every sign that she is interested in me. The Society has asked me to play nice. That means no bloodshed or tears being spilled because she is important to some, as their lawyer. So, I have resorted to using Cressida instead.

She is well-connected—there's absolutely no denying that—and she's a brilliant lawyer I've hired many times. We have lawyers in the Forsaken, of course. But we recently had to end the life of our go-to attorney. He'd become too cocky and too high and mighty for his own good. So, I've had to use Miranda for some contract work, and now she won't stop.

While I can admit she's a beautiful woman, I'm not interested in her in the least. When she touches me, even on the shoulder, it feels wrong. I have never been, and will not ever be, in a serious relationship with anyone. If I'm forced to marry because of the Forsaken's rules, it will be strictly transactional, with no feelings involved. I've seen too many people do stupid things because they've fallen in love. It's ridiculous. It's like they lose half their fucking brain.

I love only one person, and that's my sister, even if I wish she weren't so needy all the time. I thought marrying her off to one of the Forsaken members would help, but that didn't work out, and it ended up ruining one of the closest relationships I have outside of her. Thankfully, I've been slowly rebuilding my relationship with Reon, though I think the trust is still a long way off. I've never trusted anyone implicitly in my life, but Reon would be the one person I trust the most. He's as guarded as I am, and I respect that about him.

"You kidnapping people now?" Arlo jokes, forcing my attention to turn from Cressida and back to him. Her baby-blue eyes may give off the appearance of innocence, but the way she was glaring at me indicates that she wishes she could slit my throat.

When I meet Arlo's gaze, I know he's analyzing everything I say or do. He was once all about the Forsaken, but when he met Cora, that all changed. He's still very active within the society, but now his world revolves around her, and not so much the hunts.

"Just the annoying ones," I reply, and Cressida huffs from beside me. I could loosen my grip and let her get away, but where would the fun be in that? I know the minute I release her, she'll put distance between us and make it appear as if she isn't here with me, when the whole reason I brought her is to give off the impression that we are together.

She's been sneaking into events that I attend, or someone willingly invites her for who knows how long, trying to find God knows what and where I am. Granted, this is probably one of the safest events for her to attend, since only a few members are in attendance. I know she's itching to ask questions, to snoop around and see what she can find out, but I won't let her do that.

"You should be holding your own hand, then, since you're the most annoying person I know," she bites back in response to my taunt.

"Do I stalk you?" I ask her.

"Yes," she says, raising her chin defiantly. "How did you know where I live if you didn't have someone stalk me? Answer me that, Mr. Big Shot."

Cora laughs, but I don't dare take my eyes off Cressida.

"I have my ways. But you should be happy to be here, Miss Knight. After all, you didn't have to come up with some elaborate scheme to crash this event." She rolls her eyes, and I clench my jaw at the action.

My name is called over the speaker, and I realize the speeches have started, and my award is ready.

I turn to Arlo. "Make sure she stays here." I release my grip on her, then stride off, running my hand down the front of my suit to remove any traces of her.

It doesn't help.

SEVEN

CRESSIDA

"You can't force me to stay here," I say to Arlo.

"Of course he won't," Cora says. "Want to go to the bathroom?"

I nod my head, and Arlo eyes her but says nothing as we head to the restroom.

"So, he ambushed you and didn't tell you what the event was tonight?" she guesses.

"Yes. I agreed to come here with him in exchange for an interview," I tell her.

When we reach the bathroom, I enter a stall and sit down on the closed toilet lid. I don't need to pee. Instead, I need a moment to gather myself because I'm feeling a little overwhelmed with everything right now. Placing my head in my hands, I try to catch my breath and tell myself everything will be okay.

I'm a badass bitch.

Who cares that I'm underdressed and people I admire and respect are staring at me, looking down on me?

Maybe he brought me here to embarrass me.

He will *not* win this.

Not at all.

"Did you see the woman with Soren?" I hear a woman scoff, and my head lifts at the mention of his name.

Fuck my life, they're talking about me.

"Yes. What is she even wearing? If she was hoping to stand out, she is, but not in a good way, that's for sure," another woman says. I stand, flush the toilet, and reach for the handle, but I pause when they speak again.

"He wouldn't go for someone as low as her anyway. We all know he only fucks models. Her ass is so big that those pants barely fit."

I crane my neck over my shoulder to look at my ass, then shrug. *I think these pants make my ass look good, bitches.*

Fuck it!

Unlocking the door, I push it open to find Miranda and another woman standing there, touching up their makeup in the mirror. They don't notice me until I step up to the sink directly next to them.

"I think my ass looks amazing in these pants. Do you disagree?" I say as casually as I can.

"I think you have a mighty fine ass," Cora chimes in as she steps from a stall and moves to the sink to wash her hands.

Miranda's eyes are narrowed on me, but she doesn't say anything. She seems to be one of those women who talks shit about you behind your back but is nice to your face until they get what they want.

I don't fuck with women like that.

"Maybe he thinks I'm a model, especially with how loud he screamed my name last week," I chirp as I push through the bathroom door. Cora follows me, and as soon as the doors shut, she starts laughing.

"You should have seen their faces. You know he's considered to be one of the most eligible bachelors, right?"

Oh, don't I know it. A lot of the women in the office talk about him, gushing and carrying on about how handsome he is.

"Did you really see him last week?" she asks as

we make our way back to where Arlo stands, waiting for us. Soren is on the stage, accepting an award, but his attention is on me as I walk across the room.

When we reach Arlo, I stop and glance at Soren before leaning toward Cora and whispering, "I did. He threw me over his shoulder and told me to stop stalking him." My admission comes with a mischievous smile.

Soren's eyes narrow at my expression, but he finishes his acceptance speech before he walks off the stage and heads directly to where we're standing.

"Congratulations, Soren," Cora says as he stops at my side. I cross my arms over my chest so he can't grab my hands. Just as he turns toward me, Miranda joins us.

Really, this bitch is trying way too hard.

"That was an amazing speech, Soren," she coos.

"How did it start again?" I ask, and her eyes narrow into tiny slits as she glares at me.

"I'm sorry, did you say something?" she asks, as if I'm not important enough for her to listen to.

"How did my speech start?" Soren asks, and Miranda's cheeks redden, as she places her hands on her chest again.

"Oh, you know..." She waves it off.

"No, I don't," he says, brow raised.

"She didn't hear a thing you said because she was in the bathroom telling her friend how you only fuck models and that my ass is too big for your liking," I happily share.

Someone coughs in the awkward silence that follows my words, but I don't care.

Soren's intimidating gray gaze lands on me.

I don't care if what Miranda said is true.

Hell, I don't care if I'm embarrassing him right now.

He should *never* have brought me here to begin with, especially dressed the way I am.

Asshole.

"Do you think I don't like your ass?" he asks me.

I'm a little surprised he would ask me that, but I raise a perfect brow at him and reply, "No, you love it." I smile, but his mouth remains in a tightly pressed line as he turns back to Miranda.

"I think it's best you don't talk about me or Cressida again. You have no idea who I fuck, as I don't share those details. Please leave." Her eyes go wide at his dismissal.

"You heard him. Bye." My sarcasm doesn't go unnoticed as I wave a hand at her, and Soren takes the opportunity to grab it and wrap his hand around mine.

Miranda notes the action, then raises her nose and storms off.

When it's just the four of us again, I growl, "Stop grabbing my hand." I try to tug free, but he won't let go.

"I'm trying to keep my stalker close at all times," he says with a straight face, but there's a hint of amusement shining in his eyes.

"It was lovely to see you again, Cora. You too, Arlo," I say, then I turn to Soren. "How about that interview now?"

"Who said I agreed to do that tonight?"

"You said *on one condition*," I argue.

"Oh, no, you are sorely mistaken. I never said *when* I would grant you the interview." He turns to Arlo and Cora and says, "It's time I get Hurricane home."

"Hurricane?" I scoff.

"Yes, you are unpredictable, powerful, and at times erratic, Hurricane. So, from now on, that's how I will address you." He then looks back at Arlo and says, "Goodnight," before he leads me away.

"Come along, Hurricane, it's your bedtime."

"I guess we're leaving now," I say over my shoulder to Cora, who smiles and offers me a wave.

We walk past Miranda on the way out, and Soren doesn't even glance at her. I watch the hurt cross her face at his lack of attention toward her. She should be thankful it's not her being dragged around like a rag doll.

When we make it outside and the cold air hits me, I make another attempt to shake his hold, to no avail. We head to his waiting car, and he opens the door and hovers nearby as I get in.

"You can drop my hand now."

"Just making sure you got here safely." He finally lets me go. "Now, would a man who is as ruthless as you make me out to be, do something like that?" I have one foot in the car when he says that, and I look at him over my shoulder.

"Who told you I said that?"

He motions for me to get in the car. I do, and he follows me, shutting the door behind us with a quiet finality. He sits too close, with his thigh pressed against mine, warm, solid, and intentional. His scent curls in the air between us, something clean and sharp with an edge I can't name. I'm annoyed by how aware of him I am. How aware he knows I am.

"I hear a lot of things," he says, voice low and unreadable.

"I'm sure you do. So, what are the things you've heard about me?"

The car drives in the direction of my home.

"I know you've been married," he states.

"I have. My ex-husband is a fantastic man," I say with pride.

"If he's so fantastic, why are you no longer fucking him?"

"Who said I'm not?"

"I would think his fiancée would have something to say about that." I go to open my mouth to tell him he's crazy, that Noah isn't seeing anyone. But then I remember I haven't asked Noah about his personal life for a long time, until the other night when I asked if he had a date, and he replied no. It's very strange that he would keep that from me. I don't know if he's seeing someone, but it wouldn't bother me. Sure, it would shock me, but only because he's never mentioned it. Though when we talk, it's usually about Oliver, as we agreed long ago not to discuss our relationships. Yes, as a mother, I want to know who will be in my child's life, and I thought he would tell me if it was ever serious. And now I'm curious if what Soren said is actually the truth or if he said it to see if he can get a rise out of me.

"You did know, didn't you?"

"Know what?"

"That your ex is engaged."

"Sure." And the lie tastes bitter on my tongue as I look away.

"Hurricane."

I face him again. "What?" I hate that I answered to that name, and I'm sure my scowl proves that.

"Let's agree not to lie to each other." His expression shifts.

"You can agree, but I don't have to agree to anything you say," I reply.

The car slows down, and I see we're pulling up in front of my building. When I look back at Soren, I find his dark-gray eyes are still locked on me, studying me as if I'm some sort of puzzle.

"Thanks for the eventful night. It's always fun when you go out with a man only to be humiliated."

"I never humiliated you." His brow furrows.

Blowing out a large breath, I sit up a little straighter. "No, of course not. You were so amazing, making me go to an event in my work clothes, knowing that my peers would be there dressed in their finest. But, no, there was no humiliation whatsoever." I say that last part with so much fake enthusiasm that I hope he understands just how fucking sarcastic I am being right now.

"I see..." he says, and the car stops.

"Thank you for an amazing evening."

"That's sarcasm again, isn't it?"

I open the door and step outside. "Oh, I don't know. I'll let you work that one out, Mr. Know-It-All." Then I slam the door shut and stride up the walkway to my building. I don't bother looking back to see if he's watching me.

I'm emotionally exhausted right now.

I had a busy day at work, then followed it with a night where I didn't even get to eat, and my stomach is grumbling so loudly it's practically protesting. My whole body's running on caffeine and irritation. And don't even get me started on the woman who basically told me I'm not good enough for a man like Soren. *The audacity.* No one gets to say that to me, *ever*! I have worked too damn hard and pushed through too much to let some stranger decide my worth. I should be the one to judge that, not a stranger who doesn't even know my story.

Slamming the front door, I storm straight to the kitchen. The sound echoes through the empty house, matching the thrum of frustration in my chest. I yank open the fridge, grab the first thing I see, and start shoving it into my mouth without even tasting it.

My fingers are already flying across the keyboard as I pull my laptop closer, searching for my ex-husband's name, trying to find out if he really is engaged and just forgot to mention it.

And God, I hope Soren isn't right about this.

EIGHT

SOREN

SHE'S PISSED AT ME, and rightfully so.

I did take her in hopes Miranda would finally get the hint, and maybe to humiliate her and to get her off my back. But as she fumbles with her front door, I feel a twinge of guilt I don't particularly want to acknowledge. I wait, watching, until she finally gets it open and disappears inside, slamming it hard enough to make her point clear. Yeah, she is pissed, and she has every right to be.

I exhale, alert the driver that he can go, and pull out my phone. A quick tap, and the listening device I slipped into her purse hours ago comes to life.

"What a fucking prick. Who does he think he is?" I hear her muttering. *"Thinking he knows that my ex is engaged. He has no idea."*

There's the sound of a keyboard clicking before the room goes silent.

I know for a fact that Noah is engaged. I know his fiancée. And now I guess I know his ex.

The car is pulling up at my condo when I hear her growl, *"No fucking way."* And I know she has found what she was looking for. She's an expert at research, so I'm amazed she didn't know already.

Taylor, Noah's fiancée, actually works for me. I've had a few interactions with her before, but I didn't put the two together until I did some digging and found out that Taylor is with Miss Knight's ex. It also came to my attention that the engagement is not public knowledge. When I asked Taylor about it, she said Noah has a child to consider, which basically means the father doesn't want the ex to know. So, I took a stab in the dark that Cressida didn't know, and I guess I was right.

I continue listening to her as I get out of the car. Something about her voice is soothing in a way, especially when she's telling me off. I don't have many people in my life who are ballsy enough to treat me that way.

"I hate him," she says, and I hear the laptop slam closed.

I'm ninety-nine percent sure she's talking about me.

Pulling the listening device out of my ear, I step into the elevator and push the button for the top floor. The ride is smooth, quiet, and just how I like it. When the doors slide open, I'm met with the familiar sight of my condo—a space as controlled and precise as I am.

The open floor plan stretches wide, anchored by floor-to-ceiling windows that showcase a million-dollar view of the city. At night, the skyline glows as if it's on fire, with buildings and headlights blending into one another in a wash of gold and white. My living area is minimalist but not cold. There are two large gray sofas facing each other, cream-colored throw pillows positioned just so, a hand-carved wooden coffee table between them, and a textured rug that softens the space without adding clutter.

Everything has its place here. No mess. No chaos. Just order, and exactly the way I need it.

Unlike my previous apartments, I love it here. The views are spectacular, and it's close to work. But it does get lonely at times, not that I would ever admit that to anyone.

I stand there, looking out over the city lights

below, the world spread out beneath me as if it belongs to me. Yet all I can think about is a blue-eyed, sharp-tongued stalker who's somehow managed to get under my skin.

NINE
CRESSIDA

Last week, I sent Soren an email asking when we could conduct the interview. He opened the email—I know that for a fact because I have read receipts turned on in my emails. But he has obviously chosen not to reply.

I saw Noah earlier this week when he brought Oliver back, and the urge to ask him about his engagement and why he didn't tell me about it was hard to beat down. And finding out that Soren had told me the truth was a bitter pill to swallow, especially when I knew he only shared that bit of information with me out of malice. Because that's the type of asshole he truly is.

Oliver and I are waiting outside for Noah to arrive. He's running late to pick Oliver up for a trip to visit his family. Part of me wants to ask him if *she* will be attending, but I'm not even supposed to know about her, and how serious they are. While we have a great co-parenting relationship, I think we need to improve how we share information about who is in our son's life.

"You excited to see Nana and Grandad?" I ask Oliver. He loves Noah's family, and I don't blame him, because they are incredible people. I loved being part of their family, and I'm glad Oliver has that support system since all my family lives out of state.

"Yes. And Taylor is coming with us this weekend," he says excitedly.

"Taylor?" I ask casually.

"Yeah, she's Dad's new friend. She got me a Nintendo Switch," he says, as if I should know that. I assumed Noah had bought it for him. It didn't even occur to me to ask.

"That was nice of her." I try to keep my emotions in check, but I can't lie and say a little sadness doesn't pass through me, knowing Noah didn't share this with me himself.

I hear a car pull up behind me, and I turn, expecting it to be Noah. But who I see step out definitely isn't Noah.

No, it's fucking Soren Nixon.

The man himself.

The dickhead of all dickheads.

He looks me over before his gaze moves to Oliver. He runs one hand down the front of his suit jacket as he approaches us.

Without saying a word, I glare at him. The last thing I want is for him to meet my son, especially with his vague threat toward my son.

"Good afternoon, Miss Knight. Who is this young gentleman?" He's still eyeing Oliver.

Oliver smiles brightly at him. "I'm Mr. Knight," Oliver says proudly, puffing his chest a little.

I can't help the smile that touches my lips.

"Soren, why are you here?"

His gray gaze comes to mine before he says, "I was thinking you could join me for a drink."

I scoff. "So, I can wear the wrong attire… *again?*"

"Of course not. What you're wearing is fine."

"Yeah, Mom, you look great," Oliver chirps, and I pat him on the shoulder in thanks.

I'm dressed in jeans and a light-pink shirt. I finished work early so I could spend the afternoon with Oliver, since he's going to be away for the week with Noah. I changed clothes to take him out for ice cream.

Before I notice what I'm doing, my back straightens a little, and Noah looks just as surprised to see me waiting out here. Usually, he comes inside and collects Oliver, which I'm guessing is what he thought would happen today. It's probably why he brought her. He steps out of the car, and that's when he sees Soren standing nearby, watching us.

"Dad!" Oliver goes straight to Noah and leaps into his arms. "I packed all my things, and I'm ready to go." Oliver turns back to me and gives me a wave. "See you in a week, Mom. Love you." I give him a small wave in return as he climbs into the back seat of the car.

The car door is shut, and he can no longer hear me, but I couldn't care less that Soren is standing there as I ask Noah in a biting tone, "Taylor meeting the family?"

A crease forms between his brows as he stares at me and says sheepishly, "She already has."

I wave a hand at him. "Of course, you're engaged. How could I forget?" I glance at Oliver to make sure he isn't paying us any attention before I look back at Noah. "Have a good week."

Goddammit! I turn and walk back to my house, but just as I reach to the door, I look to Soren and say,

"You can go now. You aren't wanted here." Then I slam the door shut behind me.

Leaning against it, I can hear them speaking.

"Are you two working together?" Noah asks Soren.

"You could say that," Soren replies vaguely.

They go quiet again before I hear a woman's voice.

"Soren, it's good to see you."

"Taylor," he says in greeting.

And that has me whipping open the door, and everyone's attention swings to me. I glare at Soren and point at him. "*You*. Get inside. *Now*."

Soren's eyes narrow before he makes his way to me. I step aside so he can enter, and when he does, I shoot a bright but fake smile at my ex and his fiancée before I shut the door. Taking a deep breath, I gather the courage to turn around and face Soren. When I do, I find him watching me with a curious expression. He looks intimidating, dressed in all black, but his hair is messier than usual. And his lips are pressed together in a straight line, as if he already knows what I'm about to say, but he speaks before I can get a word out.

"Nice family you have there. You plan to invite Taylor around for Christmas?"

Without thinking, I bend down, pick up one of my heels, and chuck it at his face. He catches it in midair.

Fuck him and his quick reflexes.

He glances at the shoe in his hand before dropping it to the floor, then returns his gaze to me. "Assault. Guess that one is new."

"You knew I didn't know about Taylor. Was that your plan, to unravel me so I wouldn't keep fishing for a story?" I seethe.

"Did it work?"

"No, it made me angrier."

"So, you invited me in to assault me. You could have at least kissed me first."

I scrunch my face in disgust. "Why on earth would I *ever* want to do that?" I shake my head at the thought. *Kiss him?* Sure, he has kissable lips, and he's very attractive—probably too attractive for me, that's for sure.

He takes a step in my direction, and I stay where I am by the front door. His managing to get the upper hand and have me backed up is entirely my own fault. I should have moved.

Hell, I shouldn't have even invited him in.

But I was just so angry.

"I'm very kissable," he states seriously. And it

takes a moment for it to register, but then laughter bubbles up, and I lean over, clutching my stomach as I laugh uncontrollably.

He really just said that, and with a straight face.

Wiping my eyes, I manage to compose myself.

"I'm sorry, but have you thought of being a comedian?" I ask, unable to keep the smile off my face.

"You laugh, but I am." His tone is still serious.

Actually, he almost always sounds serious.

"How do you know Taylor?" I ask, changing the subject. I don't want to think about kissing him. You don't kiss the people you're investigating for a story. Even if he does have very kissable lips, which his tongue is sliding over right now, but kissing him would be *very stupid.*

And I'm not *that stupid.*

Am I?

"She works for me."

"Of course she does."

"Most people in the media work for me, in one way or another." He says this as if I should already know that. "Now, will you be joining me for a drink?"

"No," I say, straight up.

He steps in, slow and deliberate, until his arms rise, one on either side of my head, bracketing me in.

He's close enough that I can feel the death radiating off him, his presence like a wall I can't move through.

"Wh-what are you doing?" I ask in a barely there whisper.

"You're blocking the door. Or were you planning on kissing me after all?"

"Why do you keep mentioning us kissing? Have I ever once given you any indication that I want to kiss you?"

"Yes."

My head rears back. "*When?*"

"It's in those innocent eyes, Hurricane, the way they keep falling to my lips."

"Well, you need to get your eyesight checked."

And, dammit, my gaze flicks to his damn lips.

And when it does, his mouth twitches, as if fighting a smirk.

"Goodnight, Hurricane."

"Yeah, whatever."

When neither of us moves, he says, "I can't leave with you being a linebacker and blocking the door."

"Aren't you man enough to move me?" I blurt stupidly, not even realizing I'm still blocking the door. Before I can slide out of the way, he grips my waist and lifts me effortlessly, bringing me close. Not close enough that our bodies touch, but there's only a breath of space between us. Then he places me back on my feet just next to the door. He winks at me before he pulls open the door and leaves, shutting it behind him.

I need to stay away from that man.

He is nothing but bad news.

TEN

SOREN

I'ᴅ sʜᴏᴡɴ up at Cressida's last night to talk about the interview. I wanted to put the damn thing off as long as possible, but she is relentless. She's emailed me several times already this week, including last night after I left her place. She's hounding me to set up an appointment to sit down with her and hold up *my end* of *our* bargain.

I tap my pen against my desk as I contemplate when I should meet with her. I know for a fact that she's completely free this week. But at the same time, I know I should stay clear of her. For some reason, I let my guard down around her.

Yes, she's incredibly fucking beautiful, and I can't help imagining what it would be like to kiss her, but she is the last person I should be thinking about kissing. She's the enemy. She could bring everything down that the Forsaken has been working so hard to achieve for so many decades.

I've read her stories, and I know she digs deep and goes in-depth when it comes to researching her topics. She's an outstanding journalist. If she weren't working for a competitor, I would hire her myself. But she is, and she seems to love her job. However, the right amount of money can sway almost anyone.

But if money were that important to her, she probably would've stayed with her ex-husband, whose family is affluent. I don't think money factors into her decisions most of the time. She doesn't seem to be a person who is easily intimidated by wealth. For example, a woman who is easily intimidated wouldn't have stepped foot into the gala, knowing she was extremely underdressed and that it wouldn't go unnoticed. And while she'd put on a brave face, acting as if she didn't care, later on, she'd proven to me that she did, in fact, care very much. She was just better at hiding it than anyone I've ever seen before.

And thinking about the way Miranda treated her makes me clench my fist around the pen I'm holding. I may indeed have a type. But a beautiful woman easily sways a man, and there is no denying that

Little Miss Hurricane is a stunning woman, with an amazing ass.

"Dinner tonight?" Maya asks as she walks into my office. I drop the pen onto my desk with more force than necessary and look up, jaw tightly clenched.

"You need to get a job," I tell her. She gasps, her eyes going wide. "I'll get HR to find you one."

"Why?" She looks at me as if I just killed her favorite memory.

I shake my head and stand. "Because I'm not your husband, Maya. I am your brother. I won't continue to support you. It's time to get a job and stand on your own two feet. I will supply you with the tools necessary to do so."

"I don't want to work, Soren," she whines. My eyes narrow, and then she adds, "I have so many hospital appointments, no job would like that."

"I know when all your appointments are, and they won't be an issue." I wave her off.

She looks at me as if she doesn't know who I am. Her forehead creases, and she takes a step back. "You don't love me anymore?"

"You know I care for you, Maya, but you need to learn to support yourself."

I call my assistant and ask her to join us. Layla

walks in, and I wave my hand at my sister. "Find her a job."

Layla nods and then turns to Maya.

"It better pay well, and I'm not working too many hours," Maya says as she follows Layla out.

I sigh, knowing I'm a big part of the reason she is the way she is. I've always enabled her, and I am man enough to admit it. Still, there's only so much restraint a man like me has, and lately, mine's been fraying.

Beneath my calm veneer, the hunger claws at me, quiet, patient, waiting.

A fight in the ring. The sharp edge of a knife. The spill of blood. The only things that ever clear my head.

I push the thought down. For now.

Fuck. Now I have to clean up my own mess.

"Sir, you have a call on line one," Layla tells me.

I don't bother asking who it is as I pick up, and my back immediately straightens at Cressida's voice on the other end of the line.

"I'm outside your building, Soren. Care to let me in?"

ELEVEN

CRESSIDA

Walking into an office building like this isn't as easy as getting into an event. You need an invite, one I clearly don't have. So, here I am, stuck at the security checkpoint, with the guards giving me that *"you don't belong here"* look, unable to go through. I don't expect him to pick up when I call, but he does. A few words later, the gates buzz, and just like that, I am allowed in.

I'm escorted up in the elevator to the highest floor. When the doors part, I see a woman sitting at a desk in the lobby. She looks up from her computer and offers me a tight smile as she stands. She greets me, and tells me her name before leading me to his door and holding it open for me to enter.

I'm used to dealing with people who have

money. Noah's family has a lot of it, so it doesn't intimidate me in the slightest. I make a decent wage doing what I do—enough to afford my own place to live and take care of my son. But Soren is on a completely different level. He looks like money—old money. He basically stinks of it. And from all my research, I know he comes from a powerful and wealthy family that somehow lost it all.

His gaze drags up and down my body, as if he's assessing what I'm wearing today. I let him because I couldn't care less what he thinks of my purple blouse and my tight black pants. That's a lie. A part of me hopes he at least thinks I look good.

"What a surprise," he says as he stands and rounds his desk. "Close the door on your way out, Layla, and cancel any meetings until I'm done with my guest." When he's finished with her instructions, he turns his attention back to me. "Take a seat, Miss Knight."

"I have a first name," I say, clutching my bag as I sit on one of the two dark-gray couches positioned off to the side of his desk.

Soren moves over to a sideboard, where crystal decanters and matching rocks glasses gleam under the light. He drops a few chunks of ice into one of the glasses, the sound sharp in the quiet room, then glances over his shoulder at me.

"Drink?"

"Sure." I don't intend to go back to work later. I'm planning on going home, putting my feet up, and watching so much television that I fall asleep with it on. Sounds like a perfect night to me, along with some pizza and dessert, of course.

I watch him pour each drink before he turns and walks over to the sitting area, where he stops directly in front of me and hands me my drink. I take it and thank him, then he proceeds to sit down next to me. *Right* next to me.

"You have another couch," I grumble, giving him an annoyed look.

He takes a drink, then replies, "I do. You're very observant."

I bite my tongue to stop myself from snapping back at his smart-ass comment and take a sip of my own drink. We sit there in silence as we stare at each other.

I'm here to get my interview, but I have a feeling he's stringing me along, and he won't really give me what I'm after. Well, that doesn't work for me, because one way or another, I *always* get what I want.

"Can I take notes?" I ask.

"No!" He says it with finality.

"That's not how interviews go, Soren."

"I know how interviews go, Miss Knight. If I didn't, I wouldn't be where I am today. Now, would I?" He pauses with a thoughtful expression. "Actually, that reminds me. There's something else I need from you."

"What? Why?"

"I told you there would be stipulations in exchange for my time."

"How many things do you need from me before you give me what I want?" I ask with exasperation.

He takes another sip and then lowers his glass down. A Rolex glints on his wrist, and his strong fingers clutch the glass resting on his knee. I can't help but admire how good his hands look—tanned and veiny. Noah has computer hands. Soren should have the same, given his job, but he has the hands of a man who knows what to do with them.

Makes me hate him even more.

"This one, I'm sure you'll like," he says, as if he knows me.

"And how can you be so sure of that?"

"Because it's fun, and that's clearly something

you're lacking." He stands and goes to refill his glass. "So, are you ready? I'll send for my car."

I glance at my watch. "It's not even dinner time yet. What could you possibly have planned?"

"We'll be early, but rest assured, you'll enjoy it." I know this man is dangerous. He's dark, full of deadly secrets, and someone I absolutely don't trust. But I need this story. And something in Soren's hidden shadows calls to me.

So, despite every warning in my gut, I nod and agree to go with him.

He moves over to his desk, picks up his cell phone and slides it into his pocket, then goes to the door. Opening it, he asks, "Are you ready?"

"Sure." I stand and then walk out the door.

He doesn't pay his assistant any attention whatsoever as he follows me to the elevator. Soren presses the button, and we stand there in complete silence, waiting for the elevator to arrive.

I can smell the whiskey in the air between us. It's making me think of things to do with his mouth that I shouldn't be thinking about. Ever since he mentioned kissing me, I keep wondering what he tastes like.

We step into the elevator, and the silence persists

throughout the ride down until we reach his car. When he opens the car door for me, I finally ask, "Where are we going?"

"What would be the fun in telling you? I'd much rather it be a surprise," he says.

I climb into the car, and he gets in after me.

Turning to face him, I question, "Am I dressed appropriately for this event?"

"It's not an event." He smirks, burning me with his stare. I get that he's trying to intimidate me, but I'm not easily intimidated.

"Do you ever plan to marry?" I ask.

"Did you enjoy being married?"

"I did. I had a good marriage."

"So, why did you end it?" he asks.

"Because we realized we no longer loved each other, and that we're better as friends."

"Let me guess. You told him that first, and he agreed." I nod in answer. "Figured as much."

"Why?"

"Because that man clearly still loves you." He says it like he somehow knows Noah.

"He's engaged. Or have you forgotten?"

"That's because he can no longer have what he wants." He smirks again as the car slows to a stop.

Soren gets out of the car and holds a hand out to help me. "Leave your bag. You won't need it." I follow his instructions, and slide out. When I look up, I notice a red door. Soren leads me to it, opens it, and then motions me to enter before him. A lady is standing at a desk, and her eyes go wide, her lips curving in a flirtatious smile as she looks at him.

"Good afternoon, Mr. Nixon. Jake told me he'd be expecting you." She motions for us to follow her down a short hallway to a door at the end. When she pushes the door open, I see it's dimly lit inside, almost like a club. At first, I'm confused. I hear soft music mixed with other sounds I can't immediately identify. But as my eyes adjust, I see beds. And on those beds are people.

And all I can do is stare.

My gaze lands on a couple who are engaged in the sixty-nine position, the woman on top with her legs spread over the man's face as he eats her. Her head bobs up and down as she sucks his cock. My cheeks flush, and I can't help but feel a mixture of embarrassment and awe at the same time.

I jump when Soren takes my hand and then leans in to whisper, "Don't want you to get lost down here, now do we, Hurricane?" He tips a grin and then pulls me farther inside.

"What *is* this place?" I ask as he leads me to a bar where a man is sitting with a stack of paperwork in front of him.

"Jake, care to tell Miss Knight what this place is?" Soren says.

The man, Jake, looks up from his paperwork. And I immediately think he doesn't look like someone who would work in a place like this. He's handsome, dressed much like Soren, though he appears to be more relaxed and laid-back than the man at my side.

"You've never been to a club like this?" Jake asks me.

"Can't say I have," I reply.

"If you look around, do you notice something all the people here have in common?" Jake waves a hand at the room, and my gaze slowly scans the space. There are beds everywhere. Some are out in the open, some in rooms with glass windows, and others are in private rooms with no view available once the doors are closed. And the clubgoers are all naked except for one thing—a colored wristband.

"What do the bands mean?" I ask, turning back to Jake.

"To enter, you have to have a band," Jake explains.

Neither Soren nor I are wearing a band. Noticing my confused expression, Jake says, "Soren likes to waltz in and break the rules. But don't worry, this establishment isn't really his thing. No fighting happening here, right, Soren?" Jake smiles at him before he looks back at me.

"My establishments focus on pleasure with consent. I just opened this location. My other club is bigger and better known, but I wanted something more *intimate* for this place."

"Each wristband color has a meaning. Yellow means you're interested in playing but might not be ready yet. Green means you're up for anything. And red indicates that you're off-limits."

"I wasn't aware these places existed," I whisper.

Soren squeezes my hand and then turns back to Jake, asking, "What do you need help with?"

Jake glances at his paperwork and then shoves it toward Soren. Releasing my hand, Soren picks up the stack of papers, skims the top sheet, then says, "I'll be in contact." He nods to Jake, retakes my hand, and turns to lead me away.

"Pleasure meeting you," I call over my shoulder to Jake.

"Come back anytime."

I smile and take one last look around.

"You will not come back anytime," Soren says with a hint of annoyance and... *possessiveness?*

"Sure, Dad, whatever you say." I roll my eyes as he pulls me out of the club.

TWELVE
SOREN

OVER MY DEAD fucking body is she coming back here without me watching her every move. It was risky bringing her here, but I figured it might get the heat of her breathing down my neck for a little bit. *Will it work?* I'm not entirely sure, but I hope it does. Maybe she'll change the direction of where her story goes and decide that writing about a sex club would be way more interesting than a secret society no one but the members is supposed to know about. But I don't think my chances of that happening are very good. She's too clued in and too fucking smart for her own good. I heard that she has evidence stashed, and if she goes missing, it will be released. How true that is, I'm not sure, but I have a feeling that if I asked her, I wouldn't get the truth regardless.

"Where are you taking me now? Maybe a place that sells drugs?" She claps her hands excitedly.

"What about food?" I ask. Just as I say it, her stomach growls. "Food it is," I tell the driver where to go, and when I look back at her, she's staring at me with those soft, baby-blue eyes that we both know aren't so soft.

"It was a nice plan," she says, sitting back with her arms crossed over her chest.

"Plan?"

"Yes, what you did back there." She jerks her thumb over her shoulder in the direction of the club. "I know what you were trying to do. But it didn't work."

"Whatever do you mean?" I try to make my voice sound innocent, but I know it doesn't work.

"You assumed that you could sidetrack me. That a story about a sex club in the city would entice me to write about that instead of you." She leans in close, pressing her hands to the empty spot between us, as if she's about to kiss me. So close. "Let me tell you something, Soren. You are way more interesting than a sex club."

"I appreciate the compliment," I deadpan.

She straightens and then stares at me.

We do a lot of that—staring at each other.

"So, do you admit to it?" she questions.

"I had to visit Jake for a business matter, so I figured two birds, one stone," I admit. She shakes her head and smiles. I'm really starting to like that look on her.

Leaning in, I get close enough so my breath is hot on her ear as I say, "Did you like it, though, the way she took him in, his whole length in her delicious mouth?" I pull back to see her eyes wide and her mouth slightly parted. She fixes her composure fast as she straightens up and locks eyes with me.

"What about how she spread her legs and touched between her legs? Did you like that, Soren?" I can't help but let a smile play on my lips—she is good. "Don't think I forgot about our earlier conversation and how you flipped it to me. So, I'll ask again, do you ever intend to marry?"

"Is this part of the interview?"

"Could be. Depends, really," she muses.

"No. I hate the idea of marriage but support it at the same time. It serves a purpose."

"Marriage serves a purpose? Gosh, I hope one day when you do marry, you don't use that line on her." She rolls her eyes as the car stops. I don't comment, even though I want to grip her face, lean in close, and tell her she needs a damn-good spanking. Instead, I climb out of the car and wait for her to follow.

When she's standing next to me, I clasp her hand in mine. The first few times I did it, she always tried to pull away, but I like to know that she's near because she's a sneaky little thing. I don't know what her intentions are, so I prefer to have her in my sight at all times. She doesn't think I hold her hand for anything romantic, and I'm glad of that, because I don't do romance. And even if I did, I wouldn't try to romance her. Yes, I stare at her lips a little more often than I should, but that's because I really want to know what the fuck she tastes like.

As we walk into the restaurant, the hostess recognizes me and immediately escorts us to a table at the back. I usually come here with Arlo because it's his restaurant and one of the best places to eat in the city. They always leave a table open for either me or him.

Glancing over my shoulder as I pull her along, I see that she's looking around the restaurant with an amused expression. Were it not for me, I'm not sure she would've ever come here. It's not a place to bring young children, that's for sure.

When we reach the table, I pull out her chair,

and she takes a seat as I tell the server to bring us a bottle of wine.

"So, no marriage for you," she says with a grin.

"No. Would you consider marrying again?"

"It's not my interview," she bites back, her grin fading.

"I take that as a no."

"I tried it once. Why do it again?" She shrugs. "Do you bring many women here to dine?"

"No, only my sister."

"Oh, yes, your sister. Tell me more about her," she prods, leaning in as she places her elbows on the table—my jaw tics. Growing up, we would be smacked on the back of the head for such poor manners.

"It's rude to put your elbows on the table," I state, shooting her a pointed look.

"Really?" She slowly slides them back until she can place her hands in her lap, and continues to lean forward. Then she does something I would never have expected. She adjusts her position so her breasts are now resting on the table. "This better?" She raises a brow. "Or still rude?"

"Do you like men staring at your tits?" I ask, and she glances down at her cleavage.

"They are a great set of tits." She beams at me before she sits back in her chair.

"They appear to be, yes," I agree.

The bottle of wine is brought out, and I order several different dishes. Usually, when I eat here, they bring out an array of choices, which is appreciated because sometimes you don't want one standard meal. But it also works since I don't know what Cressida likes, and I don't want to ask her.

"I could have food allergies, you know," she comments as the waiter walks away.

"I'll save you if you do."

Case Notes

*He likes to throw words out at me to throw
me off. Game on!*

WHY DOES this man bring out the worst in me? I literally put my tits on a table at a five-star restaurant. I did it to annoy him, not to impress him.

What the actual fuck is wrong with me?

And then he has the audacity to order food for me as if I'm some woman who doesn't know what she likes or wants. I know what I like, and I'm pretty good at doing and getting what I want. So, I don't argue because I need him to answer my damn questions. If I can sneak in some questions in between now and when he actually lets me interview him, I'll do it.

I take Soren for the type of man who is happy living the life he leads. A woman would merely complicate things for him. And a man like him would never, ever fall for a woman like me. I would be a potential headache for him. I wouldn't let him walk over me, because I'm sure he's used to being in charge in all aspects of his life, including in the bedroom. And then there's the fact that I have a child. I can imagine that he stays clear of women with children.

So, I know this situation and the tension growing between us is nothing for me to worry about. Yes, he likes to toy with me, but we won't go further than that because of who I am.

The waiter brings the food out, and I'm pretty impressed by the looks of it. There are plates of meat, vegetables, and salad. I don't wait for Soren. I scoop what I want onto my plate and begin to eat.

After a few bites, I look up to find him staring at me over the rim of his wine glass.

"Do you intend to eat?" I ask.

"I'm quite enjoying watching you." He tips the glass in my direction.

"What about kids? Ever dreamed of having

any?" I ask as I spear a piece of steak with my fork and then put it into my mouth. I moan at the taste of it and shut my eyes. It's fucking delicious.

"Do you make the same sound with a cock in your mouth?" He throws the question out there so casually, like it's something he asks everyone, and my eyes shoot open.

I cough and start choking on my piece of meat. Pounding my chest, I cover my mouth with my hand before I manage to breathe again.

"What the actual fuck?" I reach for my glass and take a sip of wine. Then I proceed to drink it all before I place the empty glass back on the table, where he immediately fills it back up.

"It was a legitimate question," he replies.

"What I do with a cock in my mouth is none of your business," I tell him with a great big grin.

"If you say so." He takes his own piece of steak and puts it to his lips. I watch as he opens his mouth, slips the piece of steak inside, and then closes his lips, all the while keeping his gaze trained on me.

"Do you think that tastes better than pussy?" I ask, trying to shock him with a similar question to the one he asked me.

But he just finishes chewing, licks his lips, then says, "Nothing tastes better than pussy."

"You eat a lot of pussy?"

"Is this for your interview? Should we delve deeper into whose cunt tasted the best?" My cheeks go red. "No? I didn't think so."

I take a sip of wine, and he orders, "Eat" while waving a hand at the food.

"You're very demanding. Do you tell every woman you take out to dinner to '*eat*'?"

"No, just the ones whose stomachs growl at me."

Fair enough.

I fork up another piece of steak, holding back the moan this time when I place it into my mouth, even though it's incredible, and I keep my eyes locked on his.

"Do you think when you suck cock, you can keep that same eye contact?"

Okay, what the fuck?

I stop chewing and stare at him wide-eyed. *Did he really just say that?* Yes, I think he did. And he has no issues about it either. A part of me enjoys the way he talks, even if I know he does it to rile me up. Noah never talked dirty to me.

"Do I need to leave?" I ask.

"Is that what you want to do?"

Ohhh, I get it now. Soren's trying to provoke me into leaving by saying these things to me, hoping I won't chase him for the interview any longer. But that's not going to work. I see his game now, and I'm going to play right into it like I was before I realized what he was doing.

Without saying another word, I continue to eat the steak, and he sits there, staring at me with a smirk tugging at the edges of his mouth as he sips his wine.

We manage to drink the bottle of wine between us, though I'm sure I have an extra glass more than he does, and by the time the food is gone, we sit, staring at each other.

"Tell me about your family."

"It's probably best you leave now, don't you think?" he replies, standing. "Let me take you home."

"Is that a sore spot?" I ask. "I was going to interview your sister too, to see what else I can find out." His hand tightens where it's wrapped around the back of his chair.

"Probably best you don't." His response comes out cold as he waits for me to stand.

I get to my feet and push my chair in.

The wine has hit my head, and I smile up at him. "I've already reached out to her via email. Do you think she'll reply?"

He clenches his teeth as he strides quickly toward the exit. My heels click on the tiled floor as I move a little faster to catch up with him. He's silent as we get into the car, and he remains that way on the drive back to my home.

I don't bother trying to break the silence. To be honest, I'm done for the day, and all I want is to go to sleep. Possibly play with my vibrator before I pass out.

I don't bother thanking him for dinner as we stop at the curb in front of my home, even though my mother would chew me out for the blatant disregard of manners. I climb out and slam the door shut behind me. I dig into my purse for my keys, then unlock my front door. Just as I step inside and turn around to see if Soren's left, I come face-to-face with him. His nostrils flare, his eyes dark and dangerous, glaring straight at me. He's close, too close, and his gray eyes hint at some internal battle he's fighting. He steps even closer, and I'm frozen in place, unsure about what's happening right now.

He's clearly trying to intimidate me, but little does he know, I am not intimidated easily, so I straighten my back and glare straight back at him, which makes something in his gaze shift at my defiance.

Somehow, the distance between us is nonexistent, and I can't help it when my gaze strays to his lips.

It should be a crime for a man to look this good.

Fuck.

The air is so thick between us that I completely understand the saying, *"You could cut the tension with a knife."*

When I manage to look away from his lips, I see that he's staring at mine. I should back away and put some much-needed distance between us, but I'm glued to the spot and can't move. We're both breathing heavily, and just when I think I've gathered enough courage to step away finally, he leans down.

And then his mouth is on mine.

I expect him to pull back quickly, thinking it was clearly a mistake. Instead, his lips are soft and tender as they press against mine. Neither of us moves at first, and then, ever so slowly, he opens his mouth. And before I know it, I'm doing the same thing, and our tongues meet.

He's kissing me.

And I'm kissing him back.

The man I despise.

The one I'm trying to write a story about.

The man who is standing at my front door and stealing my breath with his kiss.

Other than our lips, we don't touch each other. I'm actually afraid of what would happen if we did. I'm pretty sure I would drag him inside right now. He seems to be aware of that fact, and we wordlessly agree to keep our hands to ourselves and leave the touching to our lips.

There's a small voice in my head screaming at me to stop. Telling me this isn't right, that I shouldn't be kissing this man. Telling me I should back away and forget this ever happened, or blame it on the wine. But I can't seem to do that. My tongue doesn't get the memo that my head is saying this is wrong. Instead, it keeps tasting him. And he keeps kissing me.

That is, until he suddenly pulls back, seeming to realize the enormity of what just happened. And before I can say a word, he's striding back to his car and climbing inside, not even glancing back once.

And then...

He's gone.

Taking a deep breath, I stand there, staring aimlessly at where his car was parked.

What just happened?

Do I need to stop the story now that I'm too involved?

Maybe it was the wine, and tomorrow we can pretend like nothing ever happened.

Surely that's the smartest way to move forward.

Nodding once, I step inside and shut the door. I lift my fingers to my kiss-swollen lips, where the taste of him still lingers.

FOURTEEN

SOREN

That was clearly a mistake.

I shouldn't have kissed her.

What possessed me to follow her to her door?

What the fuck have I done?

I don't randomly kiss women, especially nosy ones trying to dig up dirt on me.

I pop the earbud into my ear so I can listen in on her via the bug I planted in her purse. She's muttering something under her breath, or maybe it's just that I can't hear her properly. I listen a little closer, and I hear the soft sounds of moaning.

Is she...

No, she can't be.

But there it is again... Her moan filters into my

ear, spiking along my skin and straight to my cock. I close my eyes, jaw tightening. I shouldn't react. I know better. But my body doesn't care what I know.

"Turn the car around," I tell the driver.

It's only a few minutes before the car pulls up outside her place again. I shouldn't be here. But that sound, her moan, is still in my ear, soft and sinful. Looping like a curse I can't shake. By the time the car stops, I'm halfway out the door, the earpiece still in. I stalk back down the same path I left only minutes previously, that kiss still haunting me with every step. My pulse is hammering. Mouth dry. I don't know what I'm going to say when she opens the door. I just know I need to see her.

Now.

I bang on her door twice, keeping the earpiece in. I hear shuffling sounds before something falls, and she says, "Fuck."

I knock again. "Miss Knight," I call through the door.

"One minute." It echoes as I hear it from the earbud and from beyond the door. "Fuck, where are my pants?"

Within two minutes, she's pulling open the door, her hair a little messier than it was earlier, and her lips still swollen. "What are you doing back here?"

"Do you need a hand?" I ask, and her eyes open wide in surprise. The tension between us right now is so thick it's stifling.

"With what?" She tries to brush it off as if she were doing nothing. I skim my gaze over the clothes she must have thrown on before answering the door.

"Seems you're trying to reach a goal, and I interrupted."

"You're crazy."

"I do like the taste of pussy." I wink at her and then turn and walk back to the car. Opening the door, I look back over my shoulder and call out, "Wonder if yours tastes as good as your other lips."

She slams the door shut, effectively ending our conversation.

I don't take it personally. To be honest, I came back to ruffle her feathers because I knew exactly what she was doing. And I can guarantee she's going to spend all night wondering how I knew. She's clever, so I do understand that I have to be cautious around her, but at the same time, I've never had so much fun playing with someone in my life.

I should probably put some distance between us. Give Cressida the interview she wants while being as guarded as possible, then walk away and never look back. So, *why haven't I done that yet?* She could literally destroy everything, and here I am playing a game with her.

But I can't seem to stop.

FIFTEEN

CRESSIDA

I slept so peacefully last night.

It could've been the wine, or it could've been the steak. Hell, it could've even been the orgasm I gave myself after Soren left. I think it's a combination of all three of them.

So, when he doesn't respond to the email I sent this morning, requesting him to schedule time for our interview, I'm a little confused and a lot annoyed. I thought for sure he would reply with a time after having kissed me last night. But he hasn't.

It's near the end of the day, and I'm packing up to leave when another journalist pokes her head into my office and says, "He's here."

"Who?"

"Soren Nixon," she whispers.

I blink in surprise at her words, a hint of nerves taking hold of me before I follow her into the hallway, and she points to my boss's office, where I can see Soren smiling as my boss laughs at something he says.

"What is he doing in there?" I ask.

"I don't know. He got here maybe ten minutes ago, and I only just heard, so I ran straight to you."

I straighten my shoulders and head to Michael's office. When I knock on the glass door, both of them turn to face me.

Michael waves me in and then stands when I enter. "Soren here was asking about you," Michael informs me.

I look down at Soren, where he's sitting smugly in a chair, his eyes already on me.

"Why?" I ask suspiciously.

"He has some freelance work. I told him you'd love to help."

"I would?"

"He has an article that needs more work, and I, of course, offered up the services of my best journalist." He waves to me.

Soren finally stands, his presence taking up the whole room. "I hear you're the best," Soren says.

"So it would seem," I reply. "But I'm sure you can find someone else, conflict of interest and all."

"With what?" It's Soren who replies.

"My story, on you," I throw at him, and the room goes silent at my words. He shows no sign of emotion. "So, I suggest you use someone else."

"No, it will be you," Soren answers.

"Is that—"

He cuts me off before I can say anything further. "Good. If you'll meet me at my office tomorrow morning at nine sharp, that would be great." He doesn't say another word as he brushes past me on his way out, his hand touching my side, which I know was on purpose.

Michael and I are silent until the door shuts behind him. Turning, I see everyone in the office watching him go, and he doesn't pay them a lick of attention.

"You should stop whatever you're about to say," Michael says as he sits back down, shaking his head.

"Why?"

He huffs out a breath. "Because he just bought this place."

"He *what?*" I screech, clearly not having heard him right.

"Yes, he's the new owner and our new boss."

"So, what does that mean?" I sit in the same chair Soren did.

"For you, it means he's requested that all stories go through him for approval first."

"Just from me?" I ask, appalled by that one simple act. How dare he, just another egotistical male with more money than sense, trying to silence a woman. He needs control in every aspect of his life, except the one thing he can't control, but he's trying to: me.

"Yes, just you."

"I wasn't even aware we were up for sale."

"Everything has a price," he says tiredly. "Especially if you have as much money as that man does."

How was he able to swoop in and buy the company so quickly and without much of a fight? And why did he do it? Is he that worried about what I might find out about him? I'm sure he's good at covering his tracks, so he probably doesn't even have anything to worry about. Or maybe this is all just a game of manipulation and him proving a point that he's always right and will win in every situation.

It makes me wonder what he does to people who prove him wrong. The thought of that sends a shiver down my spine. He probably kills them. Or more likely, has someone else do the job. While I know he likes to get his hands dirty in the ring, I can't imagine him personally killing someone.

But I've been wrong about men before.

For example, my ex-husband. I thought Noah and I were still close, still friends. I didn't think he would start seriously dating someone without telling me. So, finding out he got engaged and kept it from me was a shock.

I don't care that he's getting married again. Honestly, I hope they're very happy together. But the fact that he hid the woman who will be my son's stepmother sits uneasily in my stomach. And it seems that Soren knows more about her than I do, and that sits even worse.

Later that night, I call to check in on Oliver. He tells me about all the fun he's having, that he misses me, and how he can't wait to see me. Oliver has been such a blessing, and I thank God for him every single day. He is literally the most perfect human. He is kind and caring, but he can be a little cutthroat when he wants to be, which I encourage because not everyone should be nice all the time. The world needs people who say it how it is. Noah isn't like that, though. I think Oliver takes after him a little bit, as well, but I know he gets his spice from me.

As REQUESTED, I arrive at Soren's office at nine o'clock on the dot. His assistant gives me a smile and tells me to go on in. When I push the door open, I find him sitting behind his desk, his sister seated across from him. I'm not sure if she knows who I am, but I know exactly who she is.

His gaze flicks to me before moving back to her.

He dismisses her, but she doesn't move.

"Maya."

"No, I quit," she says, shrugging her shoulders.

"It's been less than a week, Maya. You can't quit."

"Well, I did, so give me access to the money again." He sighs and stares at her, annoyance written all over his face. I know that look; my sisters give it to me when I annoy them.

"That's not happening. I'm not playing around, Maya."

"Are you interested in that trashy-looking reporter at the door? You can see what she's wearing, right? She's only after you for your money."

Surely, she isn't talking about me.

Well, I suppose that's the polite way of saying no to the interview. I'm not invested in Soren. Sure, the man knows how to use his tongue, but we've forgotten about that and moved past it like it never happened.

Soren's eyes don't leave his sister as he cuts her down. "Mind your fucking words in my office, Maya."

Maya stands from her chair and leans over the desk. "You're going to protect her over me?" she accuses.

I have no idea what she's talking about.

What would Soren be protecting me from?

"No. I've told you and warned you, and you continue to not listen," he replies.

She straightens, and her hand lands on her hip. "You can't give up on me, Soren. We only have each other," she states. Then she turns and walks past me, lifting her nose in the air as she goes. All I can do is stand rooted to the spot, wondering about the strange conversation I just witnessed. When I finally turn to face Soren, I find him sitting in his expensive executive chair, watching me as he taps a pen on the desk.

"You're on time," he notes.

"I am," I reply. "Do I call you 'boss' now?" I keep my gaze on him as I take a seat.

"I prefer, *sir*." His piercing gray eyes don't waver, full of challenge. "But if 'boss' makes it easier for you.

I won't argue." His lips twitch ever so slightly when he says it. "I actually called you here to fire you."

At first, I think I didn't hear him correctly. My brain just refuses to process it. But then he repeats it, and sure enough, I'm fucking fired. The word slams into me like a well-timed slap. Heat rushes to my face. Humiliation, hurt, and disbelief all tangled into one breathless second. I should say something. Fight back. But for one terrifying heartbeat, all I can do is stand there, stunned.

Was this his game plan all along?

To fuck with me?

Yes, he was my story, but I haven't done anything to hurt his business. I only seek the truth.

"How dare you—"

"And promote you," he says, not letting me finish. "I've read your articles. You're a fantastic writer."

For a second, I stare at him, my brain trying to catch up.

Promote. Not fire. Not ruin.

The pressure in my chest releases so fast I nearly sway.

"Thank you..." I manage, still stunned. "I think."

"I recognize talent when I see it, Miss Knight." There he is again, using my last name like that.

"Can you stop calling me that? It's Noah's family name."

"Okay, Hurricane. Any other requests?"

"Is this to stop me from doing the story on you?"

He resumes tapping the pen. "I saw an opportunity and took it."

"Okay, so why?"

"Why what?"

"Why buy the company where I work, fire me, then promote me to a different position?"

"I just told you the why, but you don't seem very interested in listening."

"Oh, I'm very interested in listening. What's the job?"

"I want you to manage the newsroom here." My eyes go wide. The newsroom? Like, where the stories are approved or rejected. He wants me in charge of that?

My heart stutters. That's not just a promotion; it's a power shift. One I was not expecting.

"What's the catch?" I ask, already knowing.

"You drop the story on me."

And there it is. The leash.

I rise, smoothing my expression into something polite. Controlled. Even as my insides are in tumult. "I'll think on it," I tell him, then turn to leave.

"You have until the end of the day. I'm in the ring tonight. I'll see you there. You remember how to get there?"

"Yes."

But the real answer is more complicated. I open the door, and I don't look back as I walk out.

SIXTEEN

SOREN

My hands are wrapped, and I'm shirtless as I look out at the crowd. I don't usually pay attention to the onlookers before a fight. I prefer my mind to be clear of anything and anyone before stepping into the ring. It's how I drag myself back down to reality.

My father put me in boxing when I was young, and I've always loved it. It was probably one of the only good things he ever did for me before he died. All that pent-up aggression I had from losing him and my mother had to be sourced somewhere, and being left to raise my sick sister had to be let out somewhere. It just so happened that someone mentioned an underground fighting ring, so I went to watch and knew straightaway it was what I needed.

The following night, I asked if I could step into

the ring and fight. The guy laughed in my face. Sure, I was tall enough, but I didn't have the body of a fighter—too lean, too hollow from skipping meals. Our parents hadn't left us with a damn thing. Even though growing up, we had money, it seems they owed a lot of people, so it was on me to find work wherever I could, scraping together cash just to keep us afloat. People are always surprised when they hear that part of my story because my grandparents were very wealthy. But my father blew it all on alcohol and gambling until there was nothing left but the house.

He'd gone downhill after my mother left for good. She'd already been in and out of our lives for years before that, though. I don't think she ever really wanted kids, but when Maya was diagnosed with her heart condition, that was too much for her. I looked for her after Dad passed, and it was years later that I found out that she had died too.

I kept trying to get into that ring for a solid two weeks. When I was finally allowed to fight, I got my ass handed to me. I went down within five minutes with nothing but a black eye and some broken ribs to show for it.

And then a few weeks later, I found a gym and a trainer named Terry. He specialized in a mix of jiu-jitsu and boxing and was willing to help me. I caught on pretty quickly, and within a month, I was back in the ring. Of course, I got my ass handed to me again, but I lasted longer than I did the first time. It wasn't until my tenth fight that I actually won, and I was fucking ecstatic.

Fighting is one of my first loves, followed closely by the Forsaken. I love both of them, each for different reasons. The Forsaken provides a safe place for me to show my dark side that I keep hidden from the rest of the world. And the fighting keeps my demons in check and helps me release my anger. I have a reputation to uphold, after all, and I need to maintain at least the facade of control.

I scan the sea of faces one last time, but I don't see the one belonging to the woman I'm looking for. So, I turn away, step into the ring, and begin a different kind of hunt, my thirst for blood no less visceral.

SEVENTEEN

CRESSIDA

This time, I don't push my way through the mass of bodies to the front. I stay in the back, watching him, knowing he's searching for me. He's swept his gaze over the crowd more than once from where he stands in the shadows near the door leading to the dressing area.

I feel like I fit in a little more than I did last time, with my jeans, tank top, and black combat boots. No one has even given me a second glance.

A loud *crack* echoes through the room, and everyone shouts. Last time I saw Soren fight, he waited to make his move. That's what he does—toys with his opponents and tires them out—but this time he came out swinging as soon as the bell rang, and now his opponent is sprawled on the floor.

The crowd cheers loudly as he stands in the middle of the ring, gaze sweeping over every face once more. I know the second he spots me because his lip twitches, just barely, and suddenly it's like all the oxygen leaves my lungs. Before I can move a muscle, he's making his way toward me. The crowd parts for him, some calling his name, others patting him on the shoulder, congratulating him, but he ignores them all, his focus locked firmly on me.

And just like that, the roar of the crowd fades, drowned out by the pounding in my chest. He's walking through the chaos, but it feels like he's bringing it with him and dragging it straight to me.

Then he stops directly in front of me. "Miss Knight." His eyes drag down my body, stopping just for a breath on my cleavage before they lower past my tight jeans, all the way down to my combat boots, and then he leisurely trails upward until he finds my eyes again.

"I told you to stop calling me that," I bite out.

Someone bumps into me, and his hands shoot out to protect us.

"You did. Hurricane it is, then. Come to the back with me." When I don't say anything or move, he smirks. "I could carry you again, if you prefer."

I know he'll do it, so I step back and hold up my

hands. "No, I'm very capable of moving my own legs."

He eyes me skeptically before he does what he always does, clasps my hand, and pulls me along behind him. He doesn't let go until we're in the dressing room, where he opens his locker and pulls out a few things. He's not wearing a shirt, and I can't help but admire his back, how toned and muscular it is.

With nothing else to do, I stand here, awkwardly, and stare at him. He steps back from his locker and drops his shorts, showcasing his perfectly round ass. Noah has a hairy ass, but Soren's is smooth.

Without warning, he turns, and his cock fills my view. "It's rude to stare."

I whip my gaze up to his face, expecting disapproval, but I can tell for a change he's joking by the slight curl of his lips. "But as luck would have it, I don't give a fuck." Soren turns and walks to the open showers.

"Why are there no other fighters in here?" I ask.

"Because I own this heap of shit, and I make them go to the women's side." Of course, he owns it, the control freak that he is. Makes sense, I guess.

"So, where do the women go?"

He turns on the water and looks back at me, his

gaze dripping with condescension, like I've just told a joke he doesn't think is funny. "No women are allowed to fight here," he states categorically.

Stepping under the steaming spray, he makes sure to face me. And I can't help how my gaze drifts to his ridged abdominals and his cock, which is semi-hard.

"Care to join me?" he asks, not commenting about my staring this time. *I think he likes it.*

I ignore the question and sit down on one of the benches. I might as well be comfortable while I watch.

"Did you think about my offer?" he asks.

"Another newspaper reached out to me and offered me a job," I tell him.

He pauses, his hands on his chest. "And?"

"I want to write what *I* want to write."

"And you want to write about me," he says, stating the obvious.

"I'm a curious woman, Soren. I want to know things that others would usually shy away from."

"Yes, I know."

He turns the water off, not bothering to grab a towel, and walks toward me, leaving a trail of water behind him. He stops just in front of me, his cock almost in my face. I'm thankful I shoved my hands under my thighs when I sat down, because the way he's looking at me, the way heat rolls off him like a second skin, his cock bobbing long and thick and almost in my face, I don't trust myself not to reach out and touch him.

I tilt my head back so I can meet his eyes, and he reaches down and touches my chin. "I'll buy those too," he says, as if that's the obvious answer.

"You wouldn't."

"Everything has a price."

"I don't," I tell him.

"No, so it appears." His hand drops from my face as he steps back to his locker, where he starts drying himself. "But we have a conflict of interest now," he states.

"How so?"

"Because you want me to fuck you."

I immediately start shaking my head as he continues to get dressed. Yes, a small part of me can't deny the attraction that is there, not that I would admit that to him, though. Why would I inflate his ego more than it already is? When he's fully clothed, he turns to me and says, "Come back to my place. We can discuss your interview."

"That seems highly inappropriate," I reply as I rise to my feet.

"Does it, though?"

"Yes, it does. Do you bring your other employees back to your apartment?"

"No," he says as he pulls his keys from his bag.

"Then, I think I should go home. Was that all you wanted to discuss?"

"Come back to mine." He completely ignores my question. His agenda is the only thing on his mind.

"No," I insist.

He steps closer and leans down so his lips are dangerously close to mine. "Do you plan to go home and pleasure yourself with a toy, when I'm willing to assist you in that department?"

My eyes widen and then narrow at his words.

After a moment, I shoot him a sly smile and say, "Maybe," before I turn, intending to leave through the door he brought me in. But before I can take a step, he yanks me back so I slam into him, my hands coming up to his chest to steady myself.

"Use the back door. It's less crowded," he says before I can tell him to stop touching me.

Asshole.

He backs away, walks to a back door I overlooked before, and pushes it open.

"Did you drive here?"

"No."

"I'll take you."

"No, I got here on my own, and I can see myself home on my own as well." I raise a brow at him as he continues to hold the door open, waiting for me.

"I'm driving you home. So, get moving." He jerks his head, indicating for me to get out.

I cross my arms over my chest. "Does that work for you, telling a woman what to do?"

His gray eyes lock on mine. "Yes."

"Of course it does. Do you say 'please, drop your panties' as well?"

"I don't say 'please.'"

"Yeah, figured as much." I shrug and walk outside, pulling out my phone to request a ride. Then he takes my cell from my hand and strides toward his car without hesitation.

"Hey!" I follow after him.

He unlocks the car and opens the back door to throw his bag inside before closing it and then turning to face me. "Get in the car," he orders.

"Give me my phone back."

"Get in the car," he repeats, opening the passenger door. "*Now*."

The voices of a few drunk people leaving the fight drift over to us.

"No."

"I *will* pick you up and put you in there myself," he threatens.

"I'll get out," I sass back.

"I *will* put you on my lap as I drive."

"That's mighty dangerous."

"I like to live on the edge."

"Yes, I'm sure you do," I say with an eye roll. To which he grinds his jaw.

He slips my phone into his pocket and then takes a step in my direction.

"I know kung fu," I warn, and his lips twitch.

"I'm sure you do," he drawls.

I don't actually know any fighting styles, but I thought it might be a warning to leave me alone. Clearly, the man doesn't listen, because he lifts me into his arms and hauls me to the car like I'm a piece of luggage. At the open driver's side door, he pivots and then climbs in. I bend my legs, without even thinking, as he slides the seat back so we both fit.

"Nope, this is *not* happening," I tell him, trying to push away. But he's strong and doesn't let me go. I'm now half in the car with one knee between his legs.

"You either get into the passenger seat, or I'll keep you right here until I get you home."

I clench my teeth as I glare at him. "You are not

in charge of me. You told me to come here tonight, and I did."

"Yes, about that—"

"Nope. We are not discussing that now. You're annoying me." I try to push away again, but he's so fucking strong.

"Passenger or driver's side?" he asks.

"Neither." The word leaves me accompanied by a growl.

He shrugs, closing the door, and then maneuvers my body so he can slide in properly. I end up basically straddling him, my knees on either side of his hips, and my back against the steering wheel.

If I lower myself just a little, I would be able to feel him between my legs. Nope. I can't think those things. Staring at him, I try to give him my best fuck-you glare. And all he does is smirk.

"Your place or mine?" he asks.

"Neither," I say again.

In response, he pulls me down until I have no choice but to sit on his lap and feel him *there.*

"Remove your hands," I demand.

"You didn't use your manners."

"Move your *fucking* hands," I say with a bright tone and a smile. "Better?" I cock my head to the side in challenge, watching his jaw tighten.

"You know what that mouth does to me," he says, voice low and raspy. Then, as quick as lightning, his hands are on my face, holding me in place while he leans forward. And before I know what's happening, his lips are on mine, and I'm opening my mouth to let his tongue slide inside.

Again.

I have to stop letting him in, but *gosh, can he kiss.* He tastes like so many possibilities and all the wrong things all at once. I know I should stop; this isn't right. But my hands somehow find their way to his chest through his open shirt, caressing his hot skin when I should be slapping him.

He slides one hand down my body, slowly, as if he's afraid he might frighten me. Or maybe he's just taking his time with me. I'm not sure which. When his hand lands on my ass, he squeezes it and then pulls me even closer and rubs his massive cock against me until pleasure starts spiking at my core, and without thinking, I push myself down more so I'm pressed as tight as I can get against him.

God, he feels so good.

A knock on the window makes me jump, and my teeth scrape his lip as I pull back.

He locks eyes with me and smirks before another knock comes.

EIGHTEEN

SOREN

"WHAT?" I snap as I turn at the sound of someone knocking on my window.

"Great fight, man. Think you can teach me?" the man asks.

Cressida attempts to move off my lap, but I yank her back. Having my aching, hard-as-fuck cock pressing against her feels too damn good to stop now.

"No," I tell him, then basically dismiss him by turning my attention back to Cressida.

"Let me go. You can drive me home," she says.

But I don't want to let her go.

I want her lips back on mine and to feel her pushing down against my cock again.

Fuck.

What are we doing?

I don't play with women, but I can't seem to stop myself when it comes to her.

What is wrong with me?

"Come on, man, I pay well," the man outside the window offers. Ignoring him, I keep my focus trained on the woman straddling me.

"You'll stay in the car? You won't try to run off?" I confirm.

"Bros before hoes," the guy calls out.

Cressida's eyes flare wide, and she turns her head to the window. "Fuck you! I'm no one's hoe."

I can't fight a smirk from forming. I lean in and whisper in her ear, "You plan to pull out your kung fu skills on him?"

I growl, "Fuck off."

The guy holds up his hands and starts backing up, clearly intoxicated. When I feel he's far enough away from the car, I look back at her.

"I have skills," she asserts before climbing into the passenger seat.

"I'm sure you do."

"I do," she insists, then adds, "With my mouth."

That makes me look over at her with a raised brow. She shrugs like it's something she would usually say as I start the car. She buckles up before I pull out of the parking lot, and the short drive to her house is made mainly in silence, until I break it.

"Reconsider my offer," I say.

"Hmm... no! I think I'll accept the other offer."

"I wasn't talking about the job." I glance her way to see her watching me.

"That's a no, too. Why would I go back to your apartment?"

"Because it would be a good night."

She scoffs. "You sound so sure of yourself."

"I am," I reply without hesitation.

"Sorry, no can do. I have my son to think about."

"You don't. He's away with your ex-husband and his new fiancée."

Her jaw clenches, then she says, "I'm busy."

"You aren't. Any other excuse?"

"I don't want to be fucked by you."

"You do, so stop lying to yourself."

"Did someone drop you on your head when you were a baby?" she asks, turning her body more toward me. "You really have a problem with the word 'no.'"

"Most people see 'no' as a final answer. I take it to mean I have to change tactics in order to get what I want."

"Well, when a woman says 'no,' she means it."

I don't bother arguing with that, because while I may be fucked-up, I agree with what she's said.

The urge to take her to my place is real, but instead, I drive her straight to her house. When we stop out front, she doesn't bother thanking me or say another word before she opens the door and steps out. I watch her as she walks to her front door, unlocks it, pushes it open, and steps inside. Then she turns and offers me a cheeky wave before she shuts the door, cutting off my view of her.

Cressida has gotten under my skin in many ways, but not in the way I want her to be. There's no point in denying the attraction between us. She could disagree about it all she wants, but we both know it's there and alive.

When I first met her, I thought she was an annoying woman who wouldn't stop harassing me. She was persistent, and a part of me respects that about her, but another part just wanted her to go away. So, I did the only logical thing I could do—I purchased her place of employment with the hope I could stop her witch hunt. But it seems her persistence is stronger than I thought.

I wasn't lying when I told her I would buy her next place of employment. I will do it repeatedly until she has nowhere left to go and nowhere to publish her stories. She's a fantastic journalist, which is part of the reason I offered her a job. I believe she can get things done that others can't, and her boss attests to that. She would be an asset to have on my payroll, and I'd be able to have a say in what she publishes. I just have to talk her into agreeing to my offer.

I pull my earbud from out of my pocket and put it in my ear so I can check on her. She's walking around her house, doors closing, and there is the rustling of clothes. Then I hear the telltale hum of a vibrator.

She may deny our attraction all she wants, but I know for a fact she wants me as much as I desire her. The moans and heavy breathing coming through the earbud are all the proof I need.

She *wants* me.

And I'm done waiting for her to say it aloud.

NINETEEN

CRESSIDA

Case Notes

Someone is knocking on my door, and I ignore it with a groan. The same thing happened last time I got my vibrator out to play.

"Miss Knight," I hear those now-familiar words call out in a loud voice, followed by more insistent knocking. Pounding my fists on the mattress, I make a frustrated sound before I rise from the bed. My jeans are crumpled on the floor, so I grab my sleep shorts and slide them on. Leaving my toy abandoned on the bed, I walk out of the bedroom to hear *him* calling out to me again. Pulling open the door, I find Soren standing there, looking way too good. My chest starts fluttering from the way his eyes are on me right now. His hair is still damp, a sexy mess with pieces falling haphazardly over one eye, and the streetlights illuminate the feral gleam in his eyes.

"Care to invite me in?" he asks.

"No."

"I can assist," he offers, and his gaze slides over my breasts and to my stomach.

"You *cannot* assist. Now, is that all?" I snap back, annoyed.

He lifts his hand to cup my cheek, and I don't push him away. The touch of a man is something I have missed for a while. And Soren is all man—rough, calloused hands and a toned, strong body. I'm sure he could pin me against the wall and make me scream in pleasure.

I really want to be pinned against the wall.

"Miss Knight." His thumb caresses my cheekbone.

He smells manly—like the soap from his shower with a hint of male musk overtones. The combination is delicious.

"Y-Yes?" I manage to say.

He takes a step closer to me, our bodies touching yet again. This is the part where I should tell him to *back the fuck up*, that I don't sleep with men who are, allegedly, mixed up with some mysterious, possibly murderous secret society. So, why do I just stand here and stare at him, helplessly, unable to do anything?

It doesn't help that my pussy is currently angry and desperate because I started something that I never got to finish. I'm totally going to use that as the reason I don't stop Soren when he moves us deeper into the entryway and then kicks the door closed. It will be my excuse when I lay my hands on his chest and smooth my palms over his pecs.

This man is dangerously good-looking. And I'm aware of the fact that he uses it to his advantage. So, I'm going to take this for what it is, a man who only wants one thing from me, and that's what's between my legs. But I'm going to turn the situation around and say that it's me who's going to use him, because it's unfair of him to use me.

But if I am honest with myself, I think we're about to use each other.

"You smell incredible," he murmurs into my hair.

"Hmm..." I hum.

One of his hands drops to my hip, and he grips it hard. His fingers are digging in as he holds me still.

"Tell me I can taste you, Miss Knight."

There is no hesitation in my reply. "You can taste me."

His eyes flash with lust as he cups my ass and lifts me against him, my legs wrapping around his waist. He carries me into the living room and then places me on the couch. I watch as he steps back, cracks his neck from side to side, and then begins to undress.

First, he toes off his shoes. Then he slowly lifts his shirt over his head, uncovering all those ripped abs. And finally, he undoes his trousers and lets them fall to the floor, giving me a perfect view of his rock-hard cock.

He closes the distance between us once more, then grips the hem of my sleep shorts and pulls them off. I'm helpless to stop him because I'm excited to find out what he can do for me. Soren eyes me before he turns and walks away. I sit there, confused, my mouth gaping open until he comes back with my toy in his hand and then drops to his knees between my open legs. He pushes them open wider, and I take a quick moment to wonder how he knew about the vibrator. Then all thoughts disappear when he leans forward and kisses and sucks my inner thigh, and I know for sure it's going to leave a mark.

He kisses his way higher until he reaches where I'm desperate and needy for him. His mouth ghosts across my folds, but when he isn't satisfied with my position, he tugs my ass to the edge of the cushion. Having better access, he can now taste me, and he does so slowly.

I watch as his tongue darts out to touch my opening. He slides it up to my clit where it twirls in a slow, small circle. My hands are clenched at my sides as he repeats the actions—the tip of his tongue nudging my entrance, licking up my folds, circling my clit. Then he circles it again, as if he's kissing my mouth. It's so hot, and I'm already melting under his touch.

That's when I hear him turn on my vibrator. And without even asking or giving me a warning, he inserts it between my legs while his mouth is still making out with my clit. I can't help but moan as I spread my legs a little farther apart. He slides the vibrator in even deeper, forming the perfect rhythm between it and his mouth. My eyes slam shut, and my hand squeezes the pillow next to me. And just when I'm about to come... everything disappears.

My eyes fly open, trying to work out what

happened, only to find him still kneeling between my legs, staring at me. He lifts the vibrator, and I watch in surprise as he licks my juices off it, and my insides squeeze at that action.

"Did you just?"

He gets to his feet, dropping my vibrator to the floor. His cock is hard as stone, and very fucking huge. My mouth waters at the sheer size of him, imagining how he must taste. He leans down to grab a condom from his wallet, then tears it open with his teeth before he slides it on effortlessly.

He eyes me before gripping my waist and flipping me around so I'm facing the back of the couch. He rubs circles on my ass before he slaps it, hard. My ass jiggles a little at the contact, then he slaps it again. It's sharp enough that it stings, but doesn't really hurt. I can't help the moan that leaves from the contact. I didn't think I'd like being spanked, but I do.

He swats me again, this time between my legs, catching my opening with his fingertips. And I like that movement even more. He slides a finger into my pussy at the same time he inserts one in my ass, and I can't help the scream that leaves me.

"Fuck, you're so tight," he says through gritted teeth.

He thrusts them in and out slowly a few times, then his fingers leave me, and I look over my shoulder. Taking a deep breath, I watch as he positions himself behind me.

"It will fit," is all he says, but I have no words. Because his is the most enormous cock I've attempted to take, and I'm a little afraid of how it will feel when it's inside me.

He presses his tip to my opening and pushes in slowly until just the head is inside. *Fuck, it feels good.* He keeps going, circling his hips as if he's warming me up, and soon I'm leaning back into it.

"Good girl. You're learning, aren't you?" he says, and I nod my head, unable to stop myself. "Now, stay just like that. Don't move." I instantly stop moving, as if my body wants to listen to him, and then he's pushing in some more. He moans, and my body locks up tight.

It's too much.

He's too much.

His hand snakes around to my front, where it finds my sensitive clit. He flicks it and circles it, but his hips remain motionless, his cock just resting partway inside me.

"Hurricane," he says.

All I can do is hum brokenly in response.

"You're going to take my cock like a good girl. Aren't you?"

"Yes," I whisper and hate myself for falling prey to his demanding ways, but I can't help myself.

"Tell me, do you want me to fuck this sweet pussy now?" He slaps my clit and then massages it with his fingers. "I can't hear you." His other hand slaps my ass, and I groan, because *why the fuck* do I like that?

"Yes, fuck me."

"Good girl," he praises, then thrusts all the way in, slow and steady, as if he knows that's the only way I can handle it right now. He stops when he's buried to the hilt, and my breathing is heavy and labored. I try to catch my breath, feeling like his cock is taking up all the room in my body.

"Hurricane." He repeats my nickname.

"Yes?" I can barely get the word out as I lay my head on the back of the couch, still trying to adjust to having his massive cock in my vagina.

"You know I plan to fuck you again, right?"

"You haven't even fucked me once yet," I whisper back hoarsely.

He chuckles, and I think it's the first amused sound I've ever heard from him. Then he's sliding one hand under my shirt and up my back, his fingers tracing my skin.

"I can't scare you off this early on, now can I, Hurricane?" I don't know if it's meant as a joke or not. But before I can reply, he starts moving, and I have to remember to breathe. It's a lot, but once my body gets used to his size, I begin to moan. He thrusts faster and harder, while his hand finds my breast, and he pinches my nipple as he continues to fuck me.

And, God, it feels incredible.

He keeps going, in and out, and my hands clutch the couch as I feel the build-up burning inside me. I know I'll be sore after this, but I really couldn't care less. It feels too good. And now every time I touch my vibrator, all I'm going to think about is how he licked it and then proceeded to fuck me with his own cock. And I know no other man will measure up to him. I started immediately comparing him to my ex and quickly realized there was no comparison at all. While Noah and I had an okay sex life, he never once made me as wet as I am right now. And not once did he taste me the way Soren has.

Soren is the man I am investigating—my so-called enemy, or at least, he is supposed to be. But the only thing I'm investigating right now is how loud I can scream as he fucks me harder and relentlessly.

And trust me, my neighbors can hear me.

And Soren?

He doesn't care, as I hear him roar just as loudly when he comes.

TWENTY
SOREN

Cʀᴇssɪᴅᴀ sʟᴜᴍᴘs onto the couch and looks up at me when I remove the condom. Fuck, she looks beautiful, freshly fucked, as her hair fans out on either side of her. Her eyes are tired and sparkling at the same time. If I'd brought a second condom, I'd go again, and I am pretty sure she'd let me. I was hoping fucking her would satisfy my need for her, but instead, it's making me crave her more.

"The door is that way." She waves toward it. "Lock it on your way out," she mutters, still watching me.

"I don't even get a 'thank you' before I go?"

She huffs and shakes her head. "That's a no."

I pull my pants up my legs, tucking in my cock—who wants to play with her some more—before zipping and buttoning them. I don't blame my dick for wanting another round with her. Sex with Cressida was mind-blowing.

I see my phone on the floor, and next to it is her vibrator. After picking up both, I put them into my pocket, and she doesn't even notice. I finish getting dressed, then say, "Goodnight, Hurricane." I wink at her before taking my leave, making sure the door is locked behind me.

The street is quiet, considering how late or early it is. As I climb into the car, I glance back at her place. The lights are still on, but the door is shut tight.

My phone starts buzzing in my pocket, but I ignore it as I start the car and drive back to my condo. At the building complex, I have multiple parking spots, and I pull my car in next to my Ferrari.

My phone starts buzzing again, and I see my sister's name flash on the screen. It tells me she's been out all night, either drinking or seeing someone she shouldn't be, and now she needs me to help her. Usually, my assistance involves money. But I'm cutting her off, and she needs to understand that. I've done so much for her and will continue to do what I need to, but only in moderation. She needs to work. She's fit enough to do so, but she chooses not to. And

I have enabled that behavior for far too long. I see that now. I plan to change that, even though she's ignored my emails about the start date of another new job. I gave her an easy, stress-free position, answering calls, and I haven't even received a thank you from her.

I get out of the car and then take the elevator to my condo. When the doors open, I'm instantly greeted with some god-awful loud music.

Which means one thing.

My sister is here.

And she shouldn't be.

I've told her she can come by anytime, but she is supposed to call first.

Dropping my things at the door, I walk into the kitchen to find her making a complete and utter mess.

"Oh, good, you're home. Where have you been?" Maya says when she notices me.

"Out."

"Fighting?" she guesses.

I don't reply.

People have told me I have an unhealthy relationship with my sister. I used to brush it off. She's all I've got. And for a long time, that was enough of a reason. She was sick, fragile, and clingy, and I let her.

But lately, every time she walks through my door without asking, something in me recoils. Like now, my shoulders lock up, and I'm already pressing my thumb into the space between my brows, like I can't hold the irritation in with sheer force. She smiles like she owns the place. Like she's owed this part of me. It's fucking suffocating me.

"Why are you here, Maya?" I stop across from where she stands at the counter.

"You've been avoiding me all week."

"Avoiding you? Okay. Did you read the job offer?"

She doesn't make eye contact when she replies, "I missed my brother, okay?"

"What did you think about the job offer I sent you?" I ask again.

"It's too much pressure," she whines, squeezing the handle of a wooden spoon. "You can't expect that much from me."

Shaking my head, I grip the edge of the counter. "Leave, Maya."

"What?"

"*Leave.* I can't keep doing this song-and-dance with you. I've given you so much, and you can't even do a little in return. The job was easy. I wouldn't have given it to you if it wasn't."

"But, Soren—"

I lift my hand, cutting her off. "I'm tired, Maya. And anything I might say will be hurtful, so you need to leave *now*."

She wipes her hands on her white dress as she steps around the counter and comes to my side, where she leans up and kisses my cheek, and I let her. "I love you, big brother."

I don't say anything back. I never do. Yes, I love her. But words of affirmation or sentiment have never been my strong point. Plainly put, I suck at them. Give me a business meeting, and I will crush it, but ask me to talk about my feelings, and I'd rather kill someone instead.

"Take the job, Maya. Don't make this any more difficult than it has to be."

"Okay," she agrees quietly, then heads out.

I want to believe she'll take the job and do the best she can at it. But a part of me knows she only said that to appease me. She wants something, more than likely money, since I cut off her weekly allowance.

When she's gone, I head straight to the bathroom and turn the shower on before I remove my clothes and step in. Lathering soap all over my body, all I can think about is Cressida. All I want right now is *her*.

And yet, she seemed more than happy to kick me out.

She interests me in more ways than I care to consider.

But she has a child, and I don't deal well with children. I never wanted any since I had to practically raise my sister.

That burden alone changed who I am.

So, yes, I'll stay away from Miss Knight.

At least, that's the lie I'll keep telling myself.

TWENTY-ONE

CRESSIDA

Soren took my vibrator. *What the actual fuck?* I didn't notice right away, probably because I only managed to get up to shower, pee, and climb straight into bed. I had one of the best sleeps of my life thanks to him. Not that I would ever tell him that. I would never let him know he was responsible for anything positive in my life. He might take that and run with it, and his ego is already big enough without me inflating it.

Oliver is due to arrive home today, and while it's been a difficult week, I've been missing him like crazy. Ever since Noah and I split, we've worked out a way to co-parent that serves us both, so neither of us misses anything in his life. I know a lot of divorced parents struggle with that, and I'm happy we don't.

I'm sitting out front, waiting for them to arrive because they told me they'd be here at a specific time, but it's already five minutes past, and I'm eager to put my arms around my son.

My phone rings, and when I see the name flash on the screen, I completely ignore it and look down the street. I haven't spoken to Soren since last night, and I'm still trying to decide whether to take the other job or the one he offered me. I'm pretty sure the position with Soren will pay better, and that's a big incentive, but the fact that I have to stop investigating him, even though I've been doing so for over a year, stings a little.

My phone dings, indicating an email this time.

I unlock my phone and read the message.

Dear Miss Knight, aka, Hurricane,

I've tried to call you with no success.

I would greatly appreciate it if you could attend a meeting with me to discuss your new job, should you choose to accept it. I have attached the position details, including the salary.

Looking forward to hearing from you.

Your New Boss

. . .

My new boss. That's bold of him.

When I open the attachment, my mouth falls open, and I sit in complete and utter shock.

Surely, this can't be real.

Who gets paid this much money for the type of position he is offering?

I read it again and again because it's more than three times what I earn right now. This amount of money is insane. Maybe it's normal for someone like him, but it's certainly not normal for me.

A car honks, and I stuff my phone into my pocket as I stand to see Noah pull up with Oliver. I rush to the car, open the door, and wrap my arms around my little boy, squeezing him tightly. He laughs and tells me how much he missed me before I manage to pull back so he can unbuckle himself and get out of the car.

"He asked me the whole car ride how long it would be until he got home." Noah chuckles as he climbs out of the car. I notice that his fiancée is sitting stiffly in the front seat. "Here are his things. You still good if I take him next weekend?" he asks as he hands me the bag.

"Yes, no problem."

Oliver walks up to me and throws his arms around my waist. I soak in his embrace because I'm afraid that when he's older, he won't want to hug me as much as he does now. They say it happens with teenage boys, and he's getting bigger, so I'm hoping we can stay close.

"Bye." I wave and then glance one last time at Taylor, who hasn't bothered to say a word to me. It still stings that he hasn't had the decency to introduce us officially.

"What should we do for dinner?" I ask Oliver as we get to the front door.

"Pizza," he automatically says. It's his favorite food.

"Done. Let me order it, and you can tell me all about your week." He rushes inside, and I shut the door behind us. When I pull out my phone to order, I see another email from Soren.

> *Dear Hurricane,*
> *Can I come over?*
> *Your New Boss*

I HUFF OUT A BREATH, then delete the email.

Nope, that's not happening.

While I place the pizza order, Oliver starts telling me about his week, then all about Taylor.

"Do you like her?" I ask as I get us some drinks.

He shrugs. "Yeah. She's all right, I guess."

"That's good." And I mean it. I want Noah to be happy, and I want whoever he's with to like my son and treat him well.

A knock sounds on my door, and I leave Oliver playing *Fortnite* on his Nintendo Switch as I walk to the door. When I pull it open, I'm expecting the pizza delivery person, so my attention is on pulling cash out of my purse.

"Hurricane."

I look up at Soren standing there, and my mouth opens in shock. He reaches out and presses two fingers under my chin to gently close my mouth. "I know I'm good-looking, but dropping your mouth open like that should only happen when you're on your knees..." He pauses. "In front of me."

I take a quick glance behind me to make sure Oliver didn't follow me, then look back at Soren.

"You should leave," I say.

"You ignored my messages."

"I'm with my son," I inform him. "When I'm with him, he's my sole focus."

"Reply back, then."

Just then, the delivery guy arrives. Soren turns to him, and as I grab the money to pay him, Soren has already handed over a wad of bills and has taken the pizza box. Then he turns back to me and smiles.

"I can pay for my own food," I grumble.

"I know you can, but think of this as an apology for interrupting your night." He holds out the box to me, and I take it.

"Don't come here again." I raise a brow at him as I step back into my home.

He just smirks as I shut the door.

Asshole.

THE FOLLOWING WEEK, I arrive at Soren's office for the meeting he had requested about the job offer. His receptionist recognizes me and tells me to go straight in. When I push open the door, he's talking to someone on the phone as he clicks away on his keyboard, staring intently at the screen. When he notices me standing there, he raises a finger, indicating for me to wait as he finishes his conversation. He tells the person on the other end to get it done and ensure there are no fuckups. Otherwise, it'll be their job on the line. Then he proceeds to hang up on them.

I now have his full attention as he stands. He strides around his desk and comes toward me. I think he'll stop in front of me, but he passes me and goes to close the door, shutting us in his office. That's when I glance over my shoulder to find him staring at my ass. He has no shame whatsoever. *Is he wondering if his handprint is still there?* It had lingered as a bright, stinging reminder on my skin for a few days, but I don't want to give him the pleasure of telling him that.

He indicates that I should take a seat. I do so, and he follows, retaking his seat behind his desk. I cross my legs, the hem of my knee-length skirt riding up just a fraction. My blouse is done up, so no cleavage is showing. My hair is in a high ponytail, and I'm wearing red-soled shoes. I look and feel professional.

"Miss Knight." He eyes me.

"I'm here, Soren. What do you want to discuss?"

"The offer I sent you. Have you had time to think about it?" he asks.

"I have."

"And?"

"I have a few requirements," I say, smiling.

"Of course you do. And what are they?"

"When I'm in the newsroom, you will not enter." I keep my smile on my face as I speak.

"You expect me to stay out if I'm needed?"

"No. If you're *actually* needed, that's acceptable. I don't want you hovering around checking on me," I tell him. "You've obviously done your research and know I'm good at what I do. I did manage a newsroom once while I was still working on other stories."

"Yes, Miss Knight, I am well aware of how good you are."

I continue listing my requirements. "No touching me or making smart remarks in the workplace."

"So, are you saying I can't bring you into my office, bend you over my desk, and spank your ass?" he asks casually.

"How many others have you done that to?"

"None, but I like the idea of it."

"I find that hard to believe." My fingers fidget in my lap at the thought of him in here with another woman like that.

"It's the truth. I don't mix business with pleasure, and I have never brought a woman back to my office for sex."

"Okay..." I stand and hold out my hand for him

to shake. Maybe I will drop the investigation. For now. "I will accept your offer on those conditions."

He stares at my outstretched hand and says, "So, that's a *no* to bending you over my desk?"

"That's a *no*," I confirm, and he takes my hand as a knock sounds at the door.

His eyes don't leave mine as he calls out, "I'm in a meeting."

"We're done," I say, loud enough for the person on the other side to hear.

The door opens, and his sister walks in. I try to pull my hand from his, but he holds tight, not letting me go.

"Maya, why are you here? You're supposed to be working," Soren says, then finally releases my hand. His sister's eyes flick down, noticing the space between us, the ghost of his touch still lingering on my skin, and she lifts her brows ever so slightly.

"I quit," she replies, crossing her arms. "And why are you in here with that reporter? I recognize her. She's the one trying to do a story on you." She pins me with a glare.

"She works for me now," Soren tells her.

"So, you're hiring any old riffraff from the street now?" Her words are meant to be mean, but I couldn't care less what she thinks of me. From what

I've learned about his sister, she lives off of his money. I didn't dive too deeply into her, but I found out they're very close. And right now, she's looking at me as if I have a second damn head.

"I was just leaving. Have a good meeting," I tell them, my eyes flicking from one to the other.

Maya's hostile gaze follows me out, and then she shuts the door with a little too much force behind me.

Whatever their situation is, I could feel the tension in the room.

And I'm delighted to be leaving that behind me.

TWENTY-TWO

SOREN

Maya glares at me, arms crossed over her chest, and hip cocked out on an angle.

"Is she the one you've been running to?" she accuses.

I ignore her question, turn away, and sit back at my desk. "Maya, you know better than to come here during working hours."

She waves a hand in the air. "But it's okay for *her* to be here?" she says, her voice getting louder and more obnoxious.

I'm starting to see the side of her that I've been blind to, the one that everyone tells me about. But I have chosen to ignore it, as she's my sister, my only family. Why would I believe the negative things about her when she's never shown them to me? Or maybe I have simply preferred not to see them.

"Yes, because she works for me. Which is what you should be doing right now," I remind her.

"I told you I never wanted a job."

"I've cut off all your credit cards, and I've stopped giving you money. From now on, all I will be assisting with is your doctor's bills."

As I shift my attention to my emails, I hear her heels clicking closer. She picks something up from my desk and throws it at me, just missing my head.

"What the fuck, Maya?"

"You are *my family*, Soren, and you don't do that to family."

"I should have cut you off a long time ago. You're too old to be still acting this way."

I click a few buttons, not even glancing her way. She screams in frustration, the sound raw enough to cut through the noise of my thoughts. When I finally turn to face her, she is wiping tears from her face. It was never my intention to make her cry, but I can't keep enabling her either. Sometimes, doing the right thing feels a hell of a lot like I'm being the bad guy. But I can't keep giving in. Not anymore.

Arlo has tried to speak to me about this several

times, but I've always cut him off. Yes, he's one of the best therapists there is, and he understands my relationship with my sister, but he also said I need to stop giving in to her so much. It's hard to do when you're so used to only having one another for support.

"You don't love me anymore?" she asks, swiping away more tears. "I should have just died with our parents."

This is what she does—pulls out the dramatics by trying to tug on my very thin heartstrings—because she knows I don't wish she were dead. I would never. She is a part of my life, and I sometimes wish we had a more normal relationship.

Now I see that's not going to happen anytime soon.

"I can't do this with you right now, Maya," I say on a sigh.

"Of course you can't, because I'm not important to you," she cries, then stomps out the door.

I get a few things together before I leave to meet up with Boston, a detective who is also a member of the Forsaken.

When I arrive and take a seat next to him, he passes me a file. When I open it, the first thing I see is a picture of an average-looking man with red hair and a scar above his right eye. He has a very long criminal history. He has a thing for underage girls and has been avoiding the law for some time. He thought jumping between states would help that. It hasn't. He ended up back in the town where he was first found guilty and charged twenty years ago, and now he's back to his old ways. But he's smarter now. Trying to hide what he's up to. Boston has been tracking him for many years, but has never been able to get his hands on him.

Until now.

I close the file, having read enough.

He will be the prey in our next hunt.

The thought of plunging my knife into that son of a bitch makes me excited with anticipation.

"He's in a house not far from here," Boston informs me. "I'll pick him up on Saturday and take him out to the hunting grounds." He stands, nodding to me before he walks away.

We wear masks when we hunt. The tradition has been around for generations. I've been told that the founder of the Forsaken had a badly disfigured face, and that the mask's design was all his idea. It's covered in broken pieces of mirror, so when you look at it, it's a cracked version of yourself staring back at you. Poetic, really.

Those chosen as prey for the hunt are usually people who won't be missed. I always make the selection, and I take great pride in that fact. And then the members of the Forsaken get to do what their darkest desires want them to do.

They hunt.

TWENTY-THREE
CRESSIDA

I'VE EMAILED Soren to let him know that I'll start my new job next week. That gives me time to spend the rest of this week with my son. Soren responded, saying that was perfectly fine, and left it at that. I haven't heard from him in two days. Truth be told, I'm a little surprised.

On the day of my meeting with Soren, I picked up Oliver from school, and we spent the afternoon eating ice cream and playing together. For the rest of the week, I did the exact same thing every afternoon.

Oliver usually goes to after-school care in the afternoons, so his excitement at seeing me waiting for him outside the school building makes my heart incredibly happy. I bank those smiles to keep me company when the weekends roll around and Noah comes to collect Oliver. It's those times that make me wish our marriage had worked out. Not because I want to be with Noah, but because I hate the separation from Oliver. So, yes, on days like today, I do wish I were still married to someone I no longer love.

I watch as Oliver walks away with my ex-husband. Taylor sits in the car, never getting out to talk to me, the mother of the boy who will soon be her stepson. It irritates me to no end that Noah still hasn't made the effort yet to introduce us.

Once Oliver is in the car, I say to Noah, "I want to meet Taylor properly."

"Yeah, it's probably time," he replies, then opens the car door and says something to her before she climbs out of the car, looking down and avoiding eye contact with me. She runs her palms over her dress as she meets my eyes.

"My son likes you, so I want to tell you that if you upset him in any way, I won't be happy. I don't care that you're with his father... I *will* find you."

"Cressida," Noah says, shaking his head in irritation.

"I respect that. I've mentioned a few times to Noah that I wanted to meet you before I met Oliver, but it never worked out that way. He's a good kid, and has good manners. I would never intentionally do anything to upset him."

"Good. I'm glad to hear that," I say with a smile. "Have a good weekend. Please get him to call me." Noah just stares at me. *Did he expect anything less of me?*

We never really had a conversation about dating other people after the divorce. We should have, because I don't want Oliver to think it's normal for his parents to bring a parade of men or women into his life. I want him to have stability. I had that growing up, and I think it's made me a better person for it.

I head back inside to get ready. I tend not to go out too much because Oliver is with me most of the time. I love spending time with Oliver, but when I don't have him, I try to catch up with friends. And it just so happens that tonight is a celebration. My sister, Izzy, just flew in for work, and she wants me to meet up with her once she's done with her meeting. She won't be in town long, which is sad because she'll miss seeing Oliver, but I get it. She wants to be at home with her own family.

After quickly changing into a short red dress and my black Louboutins, I release my hair from its bun and let it fall gently over my shoulders in waves. I paint some red lipstick on my lips and add some mascara to my eyelashes before I head out the door.

When I step outside, the Uber is already waiting for me. Getting into the car, I text my sister that I'm ten minutes out, and she replies that she's already had one glasses of wine and is waiting for me. She has to catch a flight out later tonight, but first we're going to have a few drinks together.

When I arrive, I find Izzy sitting at the bar, nursing a glass of wine as the man next to her talks to her. Stepping up to her other side, I place my hand on her lower back.

She turns her head in my direction, and when she sees me, her sour expression morphs into a smile, and she pulls me in for a hug. "Gosh, Cres, I missed you so much."

Most of my family calls me Cres.

"Same. And you should see Oliver. He's so big now."

She pulls back and smiles. "I'm so sad, I'm going to miss him. You must come home for the holidays. Please tell me you will."

I've actually thought about going home for the holidays this year. I was hesitant because I didn't want to take Oliver away from Noah for so long, but he just took Oliver on a week-long vacation to see his family, so I feel it's only fair that I should be able to do the same.

"I think I might," I tell her.

She turns back to the bar and waves the bartender over, ordering me a glass of wine.

"Good. We could use you back home." She nudges me as I climb up and sit on the stool next to her. "How is Noah?"

"He's doing well. He's engaged." Her eyes go wide as the bartender hands me my glass.

"Holy shit. For real?" she says, surprised. "I thought that man would be heartbroken for years." She laughs. "I mean, good for him."

Everyone in my family loves Noah, so my sister's comment kind of throws me. Soren also mentioned how he thought Noah was still interested in me. But us splitting up was mutual, so when they say it, I usually just brush it off. He's still friends with all of my family on social media. I see them commenting on one another's stuff regularly, and none of that bothers me because, technically, he's going to be a part of my family forever since we share a son.

Izzy proceeds to tell me about her business deal, then complains about how awful our airports are, which caused her to be an hour late to her meeting, and now she's dreading flying back. I told her that the longer we stay out, the easier it will be to get to the airport, and she laughed.

"So, are you seeing anyone? It's been two years since your split."

"Nope, not seeing anyone."

"Married to your work." She shakes her head as we each take a drink.

"Actually, I got a new job," I tell her.

"Oh, wow. Really?"

I explain how I'll be managing the newsroom, and she remembers that I used to do that before I got heavy into investigative journalism. As long as I'm doing something with stories, I think I'll be happy no matter what I'm doing.

By the time I give her the rundown on everything, we're already on our third glass of wine, and it's getting late. Which means she's going to have to leave me soon. I can already feel the dread creep up in my chest at the thought of not seeing her for a while. It's not so bad when you don't see your family for long periods, but it makes it worse when you see them in small increments, and then they leave again.

"Fuck it! I'm booking the vacation to see you all." I slam my fist down on the bar top.

She laughs and agrees that's precisely what I

should do before she says, "Ummm... what about the new job?"

"Yes, what about the new job?" a dark voice says behind me, grazing my ear as he speaks.

Izzy turns around first because I know that voice incredibly well. I know how it commands me to do things. He's very good at that.

"I'm sorry, can we help you?" Izzy asks, and at the same time, I turn around to find Soren standing there, dressed in his suit and looking way too good.

"Miss Knight," he greets me.

"Cres, you know him?" Izzy asks, not so quietly.

"Yes." I groan.

"Did you have something you wanted to discuss in regard to your new job?" Soren asks.

Izzy lifts her glass to her lips, watching the exchange with interest.

How do I kindly tell him to *fuck off?*

I'm not even sure he would listen anyway, even if I did. He'll probably just find it amusing, as he does with everything else I fucking say.

"Nope."

"Oh, don't be shy, Cres," Izzy says. "You aren't shy."

"No, she isn't. But since she seems to have lost her manners. I'm Soren, her new boss. And you are?"

"Her sister." I watch in shocked horror as Izzy offers him her hand. "Izzy."

"He's the enemy, Iz. Don't touch his hand."

"Too late," Soren says and shakes it before letting it go and looking back at me.

"I do have to go, Cres. Should we share a cab and drop you off first?" Izzy says, standing. She checks the time on her phone and grimaces. "Actually, I might already be late. I need to go before I miss my flight. Are you good, Cres?"

"I have a car out front that can take you to the airport now," Soren offers, and Izzy gives him a skeptical look.

"He's really your boss?" she asks me, ignoring him.

I bet he isn't used to that.

"Yes," I say on a sigh.

"Okay, good. Make sure she gets home safely, bossman. And I will gladly take your car," she says to him before she leans in and hugs me, telling me to come visit soon.

"I'll walk you out and show you to the car," Soren says and then leads Izzy outside.

My sister looks over her shoulder at me and waggles her brows in amusement.

TWENTY-FOUR

SOREN

Cʀᴇꜱꜱɪᴅᴀ and her sister look alike, but Cressida has a different energy about her, or maybe it's just the power she unwillingly holds over men, me in particular, that always leaves me confused.

The cold air hits us as we exit the bar, and I escort Izzy to my car and hold open the door for her.

"You like my sister." It's a statement, not a question, and she waits at the open car door for me to reply.

"She's interesting," I answer.

"Oh, yes, Cres is a ball of fun." She laughs. "She's also the workhorse of the family."

From my research on her, I already know about Cressida's strong work ethic. She's been working since she was young and took only the minimum amount of maternity leave before returning to full-time work.

"If you hurt her in any way, I will come for you." She winks at me and then slides into the car.

"That's not my intention," I inform her.

"So, what? Are you two just having a bit of fun?" She places her bag on her lap as she stares up at me expectantly.

"Yes, I guess that's it. She isn't after anything more."

"And what about you?"

"Unsure," I answer truthfully, though something in me shifts when I say it. I don't think I'll ever want more than a temporary situation with a woman.

"Interesting." She smiles and reaches for the door handle. "Nice meeting you, Soren. I'm looking forward to our next visit."

I don't bother correcting her, and she shuts the door.

I walk back into the bar to find Cressida talking to the bartender. He immediately stops when I take the vacant seat next to her.

"How did you find me?" she questions.

"I tracked you," I tell her, and she gives me an eye roll as she picks up her drink. I put my hand on hers to stop her. "You should stop drinking now."

"Oh, yeah, and why is that?"

"Because I can't have you drunk when I bring you back to my place to fuck you."

Someone near us coughs, but she doesn't take those soft baby-blue eyes off mine. The truth is, I was listening to her, and I heard the bartender welcome her when she first came in. That's how I got the name of the bar and found her. So, technically, I didn't lie to her. She just chose not to believe me.

I take the glass from her and then tug her hand until she slides off the stool and is standing between my legs. I lift my hand and place it against her cheek. She has the most perfect jawline and the most kissable lips. Lips that are slicked with a wicked red lipstick that I want to remove with my tongue.

"I'm not going home with you," she tells me. "We've done this song and dance, and I think it's time to end it."

"But I'm just getting started." I caress my hand along her jaw, and without even realizing she's doing it, she leans into my touch.

"No, you aren't," she argues, but I can hear her wavering.

Moving in closer, I touch my lips to hers. "If you come home with me, I'll give you your toy back."

Her eyes, which were falling closed, spring open.

"You shouldn't have taken it in the first place," she snaps.

"I wanted a way to guarantee that you would use me again." *And, fuck, do I want her to use me again.*

"How do you know I was using you?"

My hand slides into her hair, and I lean back, bringing her with me. "Because it's the same way I'm using you. No strings, right?"

"Fucking my boss. How comical," she scoffs, but her eyes are on my lips. "Fine. I guess you can take me back to your place." She rests her hand on my chest as she whispers into my ear, "Maybe you'll spank me so hard this time that I'll have trouble sitting."

I knew she loved it.

"Maybe I'll get you to crawl to me."

"It depends..." She pauses, eyeing me. "What am I crawling for?"

"My cock."

"As long as you crawl for me in return."

"I don't crawl for anyone or anything," I state.

"If you want me, you *will* crawl."

I want her.

Badly.

But crawling for a woman doesn't sound like me.

However...

"Let's go," I blurt.

"Your driver left."

"I already have another waiting," I tell her as I get to my feet and pull her toward the exit. She follows not just because I have a hold of her, but because she knows what is about to come.

Us.

We'll both be coming tonight.

TWENTY-FIVE

CRESSIDA

Case Notes

Nicknames should not be allowed. They cause emotional attachment. He knows what he is doing.

As I CLIMB into the car waiting outside, he's right behind me. When we're both seated and the door is closed, his hand lands on my upper thigh. He strokes his fingers up and down my skin the whole ride to his building, neither of us saying a word. The car glides to a stop at the curb, and Soren gets out while I hesitate.

"Maybe I should go home," I say.

"I think not. Get out of the car, Miss Knight."

"Stop calling me that," I snap.

He nods and takes a deep breath. "Get out of the car, Hurricane."

"I have an *actual name*, you know," I mumble as I exit the car.

He shuts the door behind me and then clutches my hand yet again. "I know. I prefer not to use it."

"Why?" I ask, confused.

"Because that's what everyone else calls you, and I'm *not* everyone else." He says it like the answer should be obvious. But it's not.

We enter the building, and he takes the first elevator, pushing the button for the top floor. Of course, he has a penthouse condo. I shouldn't have expected any less from him. The elevator ride is quiet, and I feel his eyes glued to me as we go up. When I glance over my shoulder, I note he's leaning against the back wall, grinning as he stares at my ass.

"What are you looking at?"

"Nothing," he replies, amused, as the elevator opens. He motions for me to exit first, then he leads me to a set of double doors. He unlocks them, then pushes them open, waving me inside.

The first thing I see is the city skyline showcased

against the dark sky through large floor-to-ceiling windows. He has two large cream-colored sofas with oversized throw pillows on them, and a wooden table in the middle.

He walks deeper into the condo, and I follow him to a large kitchen. The living room is large and airy, like the kitchen, and it's all white with some light wooden tones mixed in.

He pulls open the refrigerator, and I see bottles of water, condiments, and a few takeout containers. He grabs a bottle of water, then turns and hands it to me.

"I didn't come here for water," I say, furrowing my brow.

"Yes, but you need to stay hydrated."

I can't help but chuckle. Of course, Soren would say that. I take the bottle but don't open it, watching as he removes his jacket and tosses it over the back of a stool. He then kicks off his brown leather boots and reaches for the hem of his shirt.

"What are you doing?" I ask.

"Getting undressed. What does it look like?" His tone says that should be obvious.

"I never agreed to have sex with you." An impish grin curls my lips.

He raises an unimpressed brow and continues

removing his shirt. Then he's stalking toward me, and his hand slides around my hips to my ass, where he squeezes the plump flesh. "We don't have to have sex, but we can do other things," he says.

Pushing his hand away and taking a step back, I put some distance between us. "I guess you're right. We can do other things."

Reaching for the zipper at the back of my dress, I pull it down and let the garment fall to the floor. I am wearing nothing underneath, so I'm standing in just my heels.

Soren's gaze drags from my eyes, tracing the line of my body with slow, deliberate heat. His jaw tightens, a muscle twitching as though holding back something raw and dangerous. A breath flares through his nostrils before he takes a single step toward me. I lift my hand, stopping him. *"Other things,"* I tell him, emphasizing the words. He gives me a skeptical look. "I'd like you to get on your knees and crawl to me."

I take the bottle of water and then sit on one of the couches, spreading my legs. Leaning back, I ask, "Are you thirsty?" He nods his head but doesn't move. "If you want a taste, I suggest you get on *your knees.*" I wink and open the bottle of water, then spread my legs wider. I take a small sip, then slowly pour the contents over my pussy. The coldness on my sensitive flesh makes me gasp just a little. The water running down my thighs and soaking into the cushion beneath me. His eyes are trained on me, taking in my every movement.

"If you move toward me without crawling, I will get dressed and leave," I warn him.

"That's unfair," he says, sounding almost sulky.

I shrug, still leaning back with my legs spread, pussy dripping water onto his expensive couch.

Not my problem.

I'm sure he has a housekeeper.

At first, I don't think he's going to go through with it. I assume he'll just walk over to me. He removes his pants, and his cock springs free. I still can't get over how fucking large it is. He wears that look that tells me he's about to fuck me over, quite literally, and to be honest, I'm a little excited for it.

He's now completely naked, and to my surprise, he drops to his knees. *I wonder if this man has ever been on his knees for anyone.* But then I remember how he knelt between my legs. And a slow smirk touches my lips as I think back to that.

"Stop smiling at me like that unless you want me to take you right fucking now," he warns as he places his hands on the floor.

Here he is, one of the most eligible bachelors in the country, on his hands and knees, for me. His gaze is locked on me as he starts to crawl. It's quite comical, really, and at the same time, it makes me feel so fucking powerful to have a man like him crawling to a woman like me. I'm not a supermodel, and I'm not filthy rich. I'm a mother who probably shouldn't be out playing games with a billionaire. But no matter how many times I've tried telling myself to say *no* to his advances, I really can't help myself. The sensible part of me understands that this will never go anywhere—we are two completely different people who come from entirely different worlds. We will never mesh well.

But it's good to live in your head with a little bit of fiction sometimes. And in my head, I have a man who only has eyes for me, which I currently have in real life.

I don't know if he's seeing anyone other than me. I haven't bothered asking those types of questions because I'm trying not to care. We aren't, and never will be, a thing, and I understand that, but at the same time, those thoughts flicker in my mind.

Should I ask him?

No.

Especially since I want it to stay just sex.

"I'm thirsty," he croons as he gets closer, bringing me back to the here and now.

It doesn't take long for him to reach me, and when he does, I spread my legs a little wider. Then I begin to dribble the water straight down my slit. I'm halfway through the bottle when his mouth lands exactly where the water is poured. And I'm not sure what I expected, but as I hear him lapping it up, I'm a little shocked that he's actually doing it. His mouth feels warm compared to the cool water. He grabs the bottle from my hand and sets it on the floor before pressing his hands to my knees and opening my legs farther to give himself more room to devour my pussy.

This man knows exactly what he's doing with his mouth, and I couldn't be more thankful for that. His tongue works up a perfect rhythm before he slides a finger into me. Before I know it, I'm moaning, and my head has dropped back.

He continues his assault on my pussy, and I feel his fingers digging into my thighs. I'll probably have bruises tomorrow, but I couldn't care less. His mouth is a work of fucking art, the way it licks my sensitive clit, and with the way he's finger-fucking me, it has a scream ripping from me.

He pulls away, and my elbows give out, causing

me to collapse backward onto the couch. And then he's there, hovering above me. *Fuck, he looks impressive.* His tanned, toned skin basically glistens, and his cock is so fucking hard and large, and it is pointing right at me.

"Soren," a voice calls from the entryway.

I scream, searching for something to cover myself with. Soren quickly grabs one of the large pillows and throws it at me, then takes the other for himself as the woman repeats his name. He groans and turns, giving me a good view of his ass as his goddamn sister walks in.

She stops in her tracks when she spots us, and her hand goes to her hip. "You have company," she says, as if that's not blatantly obvious. "Oh, it's *her.* Did you have your playtime and get what you wanted out of her yet?" she asks her brother, but I know it's directed at me.

"What did you call her? Oh, that's right. Journalist trash." She laughs.

A flare of anger hits me at her words, followed closely by disappointment. I stand and step past Soren to where my dress is pooled on the kitchen floor. Dropping the pillow, not even caring about my nudity, I shimmy my dress up my body until I'm able to zip it back up. Then I grab my phone and my purse before I slip on my heels.

When I have everything I need, I turn to look at Soren. "Lose my number," I deadpan, then turn toward his sister and say, "You have unhealthy boundaries. Maybe you should start knocking before you walk into your brother's home."

She looks stunned that I would say such a thing to her.

"Are you going to let one of your whores talk to me like that?" she screams at Soren. I laugh, still fueled by the alcohol, and push past her toward the door.

"What *the fuck* are you doing here, Maya?" I hear Soren growl.

If I had that voice directed at me, I'd be cowering.

I know he's mad, but I don't care.

The elevator doors open, and I step inside and press the button for the lobby. I see him watching me, but he doesn't do anything to stop me, so I flip him off as the doors shut.

And I swear I see a twitch of his lips when it closes.

TWENTY-SIX

SOREN

The one night I tell Maya not to come to my apartment, she shows up. Of course she fucking does.

My jaw aches from clenching it. I can feel my pulse hammering there, a steady reminder of how close I am to losing my shit. She stands in front of me, calm as ever, and it only makes the heat climb higher. I drag in a breath through my nose, hold it, and let it out slowly, again and again, until the edges of my vision stop narrowing. My hands curl into fists, then open. Don't say it. Don't shout it. The words in my throat are hot and sharp, but I force them down. When I finally look at her, I've buried the rage deep enough to pass the calm, though it still thrums beneath my skin, waiting.

"I need money," she says, almost pleading, after just calling my little nemesis Hurricane a fucking whore. Which pisses me off more than it should because it's not just the insult, it's the audacity of asking for help right after spitting venom.

Groaning, I reach for the other pillow and cover my ass as I make my way to my bedroom. Maya follows me, but I slam the door in her face so she can't come in.

"Come on, Soren, *please*." She bangs her hand on the door, her voice dipping into that familiar, sugar-coated desperation she uses when she wants something. The sound grates on my last nerve, but I refuse to give her the satisfaction of a response right away. Instead, I snag a pair of pants from a drawer, take my time to slide them up my legs, and then open the door.

"Fuck off, Maya. I'm this close"—I pinch my fingers together, a sliver of space between them—"to cutting all ties with you."

Her expression twists with shock and hurt, the weight of my words hitting her like a slap she never saw coming. Not once have I ever spoken to her that way. I've always measured my words, softened my tone, and done everything I could to protect her from the truth. But that's precisely the problem, isn't it?

All this carefulness has only taught her that she can say whatever she wants without consequence. And if I keep letting it slide, if I keep protecting her, it'll never stop.

"*Leave.* You've already fucked up my night," I tell her. "And I have to prepare for tomorrow night."

"What's so important about tomorrow?" she asks. "Is it *more important* than me?" The sad puppy-dog eyes she gives me usually work—they always do.

Not tonight.

I'm mad that Cressida left.

Mad that I didn't get more than a taste.

Just enough to ruin me for anything else right now.

Fuck.

I want Cressida.

I wonder if it's too late to chase her down, bring her back, and make her crawl to me like I wanted in the first place.

Jesus, I actually crawled to her.

Who the fuck am I becoming?

And why?

"If you want money, Maya, *earn it*. Take the other fucking job." I walk to the door and hold it open, and when she turns to face me, tears are glistening in her eyes.

No fucking way.

Not happening.

"Take the job, Maya," I tell her again. This time, not as harshly.

"I don't want to work," she whines.

"Too bad. You either work or end up on the street. Your choice." I nod toward the door.

"Please, brother. *Please?*"

"*Leave.*" I groan again.

"It's *her*. Now that you're seeing *her*, you no longer want to support me anymore. Why?"

"Cressida has *nothing* to do with this," I grit. "And you know it."

"This is unfair." She storms past me into the hall-way, then stabs her finger on the elevator button.

"Give me my key back." I hold out my hand, palm up, waiting.

She folds her arms, glaring. "No."

"*Maya*," I say, tone assertive.

"You give me a thousand, and I will give it back." Her grin widens, smug and satisfied.

Rage spikes. I see red and slam the door hard enough to make the frame shake.

Rubbing a hand down my face, I pick up my phone and check Cressida's tracker, glad when I see her back at her place.

Tomorrow night...
I'll hunt.

TWENTY-SEVEN

CRESSIDA

I HATE days when I don't have my son.

I'm bored, and I'd rather be doing things with him. So, instead, I do the everyday mundane things like cleaning the house, going grocery shopping, and hoping no one I know sees me because I'm wearing lounge pants with a shirt that has seen better days.

"I really don't know what he sees in you." I freeze while choosing a bag of popcorn. *Surely, that comment wasn't directed at me?* I make my selection, then toss it into the cart, not giving the speaker another thought. But the voice continues, "Oh, so you're pretending not to hear me. That's nice. Real trashy of you." She scoffs.

I turn toward the voice. Maya stands behind me, still as glass, her head tilted slightly to one side. She's as pristine and put together as ever, but her eyes are bright and wild, locked on me with unnerving precision. She doesn't blink. A slow smile curls her mouth, wrong somehow, like she's savoring a thought she shouldn't be having. How did having sex with Soren end up with me dealing with his crazy sister? I mean, a crazy ex is one thing, but this is a new level of weird.

"Can I help you?" I ask, confused about this confrontation.

"I see it, you know. You think because you're fucking him that you have some type of claim to him?"

I can't help the burst of laughter that leaves me. I wave a hand in front of my face to stop myself. "I'm sorry. But do you realize you sound like a villainous ex-girlfriend right now? I mean, I guess some people like to keep it in the family, but I didn't think Soren was like that."

"He's not. *We're* not. We're all the other has. And I don't want some bitch with shiny black hair fucking it up."

"Well, first, thank you for the compliment. Second, who the hell is trying to fuck up your relationship with him? Is there more to this than you're letting on?" I raise a brow, and my phone chooses that moment to ring.

Seeing that it's Soren's name on the screen, I ignore it and glance back at Maya. "Look, I'm going to make this easy for you. You can have your brother. Go and do bad things together because I never will again. Especially now that I see how crazy your family really is."

Another shopper walks past, eyeing us in annoyance since we're blocking almost the whole aisle, and I shoot her a smile as I reach behind me for another bag of popcorn. I'm going to need several bags of that tonight to get past all of this. Chocolate too, maybe!

Maya's phone goes off with an absurdly loud ringtone.

I turn away, intending to continue my shopping, but she answers the call, and I hear Soren's voice on the other end. She pulls her phone away from her ear and holds it out to me with a death glare.

"I'm not touching that." I give her a little wave and then walk away.

Fuck, that family is crazy.

When I get out of the cab, arms full of grocery bags, I see Soren standing at my front door. I don't acknowledge him as I approach, but he's blocking me from entering. I juggle the bags, trying to get my keys from my purse, and without a word, he takes all the bags from me.

I huff in exasperation at the gesture.

"You're ignoring me," he states.

"I think it's best that way," I tell him as I unlock the door. I turn around to take the bags back from him and note he's dressed in all black. But it's not a suit; he's wearing a leather jacket and black jeans.

"I disagree," he says.

"Thanks for holding the bags for me. Have a good life. Bye, now." I go to take the bags back, but he moves them out of my reach and then steps around me into my home, heading straight to the kitchen, where he sets them on the counter before he faces me.

"Our conversation isn't done." His tone brooks no argument.

"Your sister has a habit of interrupting our visits. Will she pop through my door any minute now?"

"I should hope not."

"Good. Because if she enters my home without an invitation, I will stab her." I beam at him, and his jaw clenches. "But we won't have to worry about that from now on, will we? Because you and I are nothing outside of our working relationship, so please inform her of that so she stops following me."

His phone rings, and he glances at the watch on his wrist.

"I can't do this now. I have somewhere I need to be. But we are *not* done." Soren steps in close, stopping just inches from me. His presence fills the space, all heat and command. Then he reaches past me, his arm brushing mine as he grabs at something on the counter before pulling back. I frown, unsure what that was about, but he's already turning for the door, so I let it go.

After he's gone, I shut and lock it, my heart still pounding. When I return to the kitchen to put the groceries away, I spot the empty spot where my key should be.

That bastard took it.

TWENTY-EIGHT
SOREN

THE HUNT IS ALWAYS HIGHLY ANTICIPATED by the members of the Forsaken. The bi-annual event gives us the opportunity to unleash our darker sides and let our demons out to play.

Tonight's chosen prey is currently on his knees at the edge of the private forest owned by the Forsaken. His head is covered with a black sack, and his hands are tied behind his back. He's sobbing, begging to be set free. He will be. He just isn't aware of what will follow.

The prey isn't intended to come out of the hunt alive.

Only one person has ever survived being our target—Reon's wife, Lilith.

Reon approaches me, stopping at my side. He's

still upset and angry at me for what happened with his wife, but I guess I can't blame him for that. Boston is leaning against his car, and we remain quiet as the other members stand in groups nearby.

I was late getting here tonight.

I'm *never* late.

Usually, the prey is off and running by now.

"Derrick," I say the prey's name, and everyone puts on their masks as I step toward the trembling man. When I remove the sack from his head, his green eyes are wild as he looks around. *What does he think of the situation he's found himself in?*

His gaze finally lands on me, the only one without a mask, and his eyes are pleading before his mouth even moves. "Man, let me go. I can give you anything you want. Just... please, let me go."

Boston comes to stand beside me, and he hands me a file folder. I dump the papers on the ground in front of Derrick, and he quickly scans them before looking back up at me.

"That's not me. I was framed," he insists.

A stupid person might believe him, but I am not a stupid person.

I stare down at him in silence, not feeling like arguing with him about his actions. He's already been convicted of the crimes I just laid in front of him. The evidence is there in black and white, and he can't hide from it.

After pulling out the knife from my back pocket, I slice through the ties that bind his hands. The second he's free, he stands. I watch as he looks around, realizing his only means of escape is through the forest.

Some prey beg for their lives before they even get to that point, but he immediately turns and runs. Which is good—it means the fun can begin sooner.

Reon stands behind us with his weapon of choice, an axe. He is what you would call a master of the hunts. If he's participating, he usually wins.

But not this time.

This time, I have pent-up frustration I need to take out.

I pull out my pack of cigarettes, light one, and place the packet back in my pocket. I'm not much of a smoker, but sometimes, when the urge strikes, I like the way it tastes.

And the thing I like the taste of best is not here.

Silence fills the field where we wait, giving Derrick a head start.

The hunt, the game, is about to begin, and every member standing here is excited. It electrifies the air around us.

Cracking my neck and blowing out a puff of smoke, I toss the cigarette on the ground and crush it under my black boot. The members gather around me while I slide on my mask. The only light comes from the half-moon hanging in the sky, so it's not as bright as we like.

But it will do.

"In the shadows, we hunt. In the night, we kill," I say, and everyone repeats the words.

The quietness takes hold once again, and we all turn and start walking to the edge of the forest. Even with our masks in place, I can tell each member apart by what weapon they carry. I use no weapon, which is what I prefer. I like the feeling of breaking a neck with my bare hands. It's a rush that I don't often feel in the ring when I fight, because killing a man in an underground fighting ring is illegal. And while what we're doing right now is highly illegal, we are removing scum from the earth. So, I suppose the hunt could, in a morbid way, be considered a service to the world.

Granted, most normal people don't have the urge to kill people, unlike the members of the Forsaken. But we've found a way to quiet that urge by hunting the worst of the worst and sometimes, just sometimes, those that fucking piss me off.

Dried grass crunches under my boots as I stop just outside the forest. Everyone else has already taken off into the darkness of the trees, and I'm left standing here alone. I consider lighting another cigarette, but then a twig snaps to my left. Turning my head in the direction of the sound, I see someone lying on the ground about twenty yards away.

How dumb can you be?

I always hang back for a few minutes, and this is one of the reasons I do. None of the cars have keys in them, but if the prey knows how to hotwire a car, it could be a problem.

I turn my back on the person and walk toward the trees. It's dark, so he doesn't actually see me stop behind a thick trunk, but I watch him as he makes his way to the cars. I consider lighting another smoke and watching him for a while because the members will be annoyed if I kill him so early on in this hunt.

As I observe him, it hits me that I don't really want to be here.

I would rather be with Cressida.

And that thought is so fucking maddening.

Annoyed with where my thoughts have strayed, I step out from my hiding spot and approach the makeshift parking lot. I see Derrick pick up a rock and use it to break a window on one of the cars. It shatters, and he immediately sticks his hand through the jagged opening to unlock the door. He pulls the door open, slides inside, and shuts the door behind him. Then he leans down like he's checking the floor, or under the dashboard.

Maybe this fucker can hotwire a car.

He doesn't notice me as I sneak closer, pick up the rock he dropped, and smash it into the side of his head. It's a good-sized rock, and I struck him hard with it, so it leaves a gash on his temple. Blood flows freely from the wound, and he raises his hand to press it against the cut.

With him distracted, I wrench open the car door, haul him out, and drop him to the ground at my feet. Because of my mask, he doesn't know who is leaning over him.

"You thought you were clever," I say with a smile he can't see.

"P-Please. I can p-pay you," Derrick stammers as he tries to get up.

I put my foot on his chest to hold him down.

"I don't need your money." Maybe if I were a lesser man, I would take his bribe and then kill him. But I can't be persuaded by money. I have more than enough of my own and don't need it. It's one of my strengths—knowing how to make money.

I press my foot down hard onto his chest until I hear a cracking sound. He wraps his bloody hands around my foot, trying to push it away. But I don't budge.

"Please. *Please.*" The photographs from his file, the ones of him with young women, still lay scattered nearby. Those women probably uttered those exact same words to him.

Bastard.

He tries to catch his breath when I lift my foot from him, but I'm pretty sure I've broken some of his ribs. He struggles as he tries to stand, hunched over in pain. But he's in flight mode, which means he's trying to get the fuck out of here, no matter how injured he is. Before he can take a single step, I move up behind him and wrap my hands around his neck.

Then I squeeze.

And then I squeeze even harder.

He struggles to breathe, lungs wheezing, as his hands claw at mine. But I won't let go, even when he attempts to slam the back of his head into my face. I simply tighten my grip. Until his movements start to slow and weaken. I know the second the fight is gone from him, when his hands fall away from mine, and his body sags in my hold. I let go of him and step back as he falls to the ground.

Standing over him, I pull out my pocket knife, kneel beside him, then stab the blade straight into his jugular. We aren't here to give mercy. There is no mercy left to give for pieces of shit like him. We're here to take life.

Some believe it's not our place to decide who lives and who dies; that it's in the hands of God. But I believe that God isn't doing a good enough job.

TWENTY-NINE

CRESSIDA

WHEN AN INTRUDER BREAKS into your house, you don't expect them to swear as they stumble around in the dark.

I bolt upright in my bed at the sound, but when the voice registers, I know exactly who it is. I should have expected he would come—even though I told him that we're done—but how did he get in? Then the sleepiness lifts from my mind, and I remember he stole my house key.

Grabbing the vase on my nightstand, I quietly get out of bed and pad into the hallway. I obviously know the layout of my house better than he does, so the darkness doesn't affect me as much as it does him.

I hear his footsteps getting closer. When I think

he's close enough, I throw the vase, and smile when I listen to it crack against his head and then shatter on the floor.

Fuck, I loved that vase.

"Jesus Christ! What the fuck?" he bellows, and I switch on the light, only to find Soren standing there with his hand over his bleeding mouth.

Crossing my arms over my chest, I stare at him. "What did you think would happen when you broke into my house in the middle of the night?" I scoff, throwing my hands up in the air as I raise my brows at him. He's wearing the same clothes from earlier, but he no longer has the jacket on.

He wipes his lip with the back of his hand, then swipes it with his tongue. His eyes, currently a stormy dark gray, narrow at me. And I remember I went to bed in just a baggy T-shirt, with no underwear or bra. I wasn't expecting an intruder tonight, and since no one else is here, I wanted to be super comfortable. Little did I know that I'd be in this situation. However, I should have known, seeing as he took my damn key.

"Well, I was hoping to wake you up with my mouth between your legs." He licks his lips again. "I must say, I prefer the taste of you over my own blood." He smirks.

Groaning, I look down at the mess on the floor, which I'll now have to clean up. "That was my favorite vase," I grumble. "Do you have any idea how expensive that was?"

"You mean the vase *you* threw at *my* head?"

"Yes, that one. I loved it."

"Yeah, well, it didn't love me."

"No, which makes me love it even more," I say, grinning.

He moves to come closer, and I hold up a hand to stop him. "Um, no. What are you doing? Do I need to call the police?"

"I know the police."

"I'm sure you do." I roll my eyes. "You can leave now, unless you want the next item thrown at your head to be sharper."

"I told you our conversation wasn't over," he growls.

I move past him and into the kitchen, and he stalks after me.

"I don't agree with you ending whatever is between us." He reaches for me, and at the same time, I grab a fork from the counter. He eyes it for a moment, then his gaze meets mine. "Do you plan to stab me with that?"

"Yes, I do. If you don't leave." I hit him with a bright smile.

He pauses, raising a skeptical brow at my fork, then steps toward me. His hand slides along the countertop as he comes closer. Once he's within arm's reach, I don't think twice before quickly bringing my hand down, stabbing the fork into his hand. Soren has fast reflexes, but I think the issue here is that he thought I wouldn't actually do it.

He assumed I was bullshitting.

I was not.

He woke me up in the dead of the night.

Broke into my house.

Caused me to break my beautiful vase.

Then didn't leave when I told him to.

So, to be fair, he has brought this all upon himself.

The fork makes a strange sound when it slams into his skin, a growl leaves my mouth—"*fuck*"—and we both stare at it for a few beats. But then I quickly pull my hand away, leaving the fork embedded in his flesh.

"Did you just…" He yanks the utensil from his hand as if it were nothing and holds it up between us. "I think you lost something." He offers it to me, and I take it. My gaze flicks to the four small puncture wounds that are welling with blood.

He glances down at the fork punctures stark against his skin. His silver eyes lock onto mine, dark and unreadable. "You really don't want me to stay?" His voice is low, calm only in volume, but edged with something sharp, dangerous, and barely restrained.

"No," I reply without hesitation.

He leans in just slightly, a slow, deliberate movement. "Why?"

That single word carries more than curiosity; it's raw, fragile, the faintest crack in his armor. I see it, the vulnerability beneath the hardness. But it's still there, cold and dangerous, ready to snap if pushed too far.

"Because I don't have room for crazy in my life right now. I'm raising a son, or did you forget that?"

"He's with his father," he tells me, like I don't already know.

"Yes, and I'm tired. You woke me up," I remind him. "When Oliver isn't here, I like to catch up on sleep."

"Can I sleep with you?" he asks.

"No." I glance down at his hand and then meet his eyes again. "You should leave."

"Why?"

"I told you already."

"No. Why can't I stay?"

"You're a smart man, Soren." Everyone knows how smart he is. He wouldn't be so successful if he weren't. "But you have issues that I don't want to deal with. Namely, your sister."

He scrubs a hand down his face, then licks his split lip. "She's a problem, I get that. But she was sick for so long that it came naturally for me to take care of her. We didn't have anyone else. I've raised her since I was eighteen," he tells me. I knew all this from my research, but hearing him say it out loud is entirely different, like something shifting in the air between us. "I see that I've enabled her bad behavior, and I've been trying to fix it."

"Good. Why don't you focus on that and leave me alone? She thinks I'm the reason for your sudden change of heart when it comes to her."

"You are." His voice is steady. Certain. There's no softness, just a fact laid bare.

My head jerks back in surprise. *"What?"*

"You *are* the reason. I realized it because of you."

The words hang there. I swallow, forcing my voice steady. "Okay, well, don't tell her that."

I catch myself staring at his hand, then quickly look away. Something in the way he's letting me in, the rare crack in his armor, stays with me longer than I want.

"I won't," he assures me.

"You aren't staying," I remind him. He smirks, and I can't help but stare at him. He has a busted lip, his hand is bleeding, and he's still the most handsome man I have ever seen.

Fuck him and his good looks.

"What about a goodnight kiss?" he asks.

"No, thank you. You're bleeding."

"I wouldn't care if you were bleeding." His gaze drops to my bare thighs.

"That's disgusting," I sneer.

"What? It's extra flavor."

"Okay, that's enough! You're getting out of hand now and need to leave." I point toward the front door, which is shut and locked. *Well, I guess it was nice of him to lock it again after breaking in.*

"Just a small goodnight kiss," he prods as he inches closer. I spot a knife beside the sink, but this time he knows I'm not playing, and he blocks my path to it. "Now, now, Hurricane. No more stabbing your lover."

"*Lover?*" I scoff.

"Please, let me stay," he says again.

"I didn't know you knew that word."

"I don't usually have to use it, so it's not in my vocabulary," he admits. This time, when he reaches for me, I let him, and his arm slides around my waist.

"I'm not fucking you. I'm tired and want to sleep," I inform him.

"I'll just sleep next to you," he promises, then leans down and nuzzles into my neck.

Goddammit! It feels good, and it takes me a beat before I push him away.

"No touching either," I assert.

"I want to hold you," he argues.

"*Fine*. Only holding." I keep giving in, and I can't help myself.

"Okay." He drops a kiss behind my ear before he pulls back and leads me to my room.

He releases my hand, and I climb into bed and get under the covers. The lights aren't on, but I can still see him perfectly as he undresses—first his boots and socks, then his shirt, and lastly his jeans.

In just his boxers, he goes into the bathroom, and I hear the shower run for a few minutes before he comes out with a towel wrapped low around his waist and a bandage on his hand. He pauses, looking at me, before he drops the towel and comes around to my side of the bed. Soren lifts the covers and practically climbs in on top of me. I have to scoot over to make room for him. His arms wrap around me without hesitation, and I let him hold me like the doll he wants me to be.

"Soren."

"Hmm..." I can tell he's tired.

Maybe all he wants is someone to sleep next to.

"Why are you really here?"

"I don't know," he answers. "But I like that I am." Without thinking, I take his hand and hold it. He flinches at my touch but doesn't pull away. His hand squeezes mine, and we lie in complete silence as we both drift off to sleep.

And I hate to admit it.

But it ends up being one of the best nights' sleep I've had since... well, forever.

THIRTY

SOREN

Soren

She's awake, and she's trying to wriggle from my hold.

"Just a little longer," I say sleepily, content to just hold her. Even after she stabbed me, it's still where I want to be.

"I can't. Someone's here," she whispers and tries to pull away again. This time, I let her go, even though I don't want to.

She slips out into the hall, and I hear her say, "Noah?"

"Hey. Oliver and I are just popping by to get his tablet. He was upset that he forgot it."

"Give me a second, okay? I just need to get dressed." Cressida steps back into the bedroom and shuts the door. She looks around frantically, then scoops up my clothes and throws them in her closet, and points to me. "You. Under the bed. *Now*," she whisper-shouts.

"What? No way."

"*Now*, Soren." The words come out in a hiss. "My son is here. And I told you to go home last night."

Reluctantly, I get out of bed, and her gaze falls to my very hard cock.

"*Go*." She waves a hand, and I lower to the floor and climb under her fucking bed like I'm a teenager hiding from her damn parents. My cock hits the underside of the bed, and I have to readjust it before I slide completely under. Just as I get my whole body wedged into the tight space, the door opens, and her son runs in. He throws himself onto her bed and then proceeds to jump on it.

Fuck.

The bed dips with his bouncing, brushing the tip of my cock.

I swear to God if that mattress breaks my cock...

"Did you find your tablet?" Her voice has changed; it's now sweet and low.

"Yep. Just came to kiss you goodbye." He hops from the bed, and I see a pair of small sock-covered feet move toward her.

I hear her kiss him, then she says, "All right. Well, I'll see you tomorrow, okay?" The sound of another kiss. "I love you."

"Yep. I love you, too, Mom," he replies, then hurries out the door. She follows and shuts the door behind them, and I stay under the fucking bed like some kind of criminal.

A shitty criminal at that.

And let's be real, I'm no amateur criminal.

She has a brief, muffled conversation with her ex-husband before I hear the click of a door. I listen closely for a couple of minutes, unsure if I should get out from under the bed. My ass is getting cold and sore, and I really need to fucking take a piss.

When my phone starts ringing loudly, the bedroom door opens, and I see her feet before she says, "Oh, I forgot you were there. You can come out now. They left like ten minutes ago."

I shimmy out, and when I get to my feet, she's standing there, clutching a coffee cup and trying to hold back her smile. She's failing.

She glances down at my now-deflated cock. "It's red." She points to the tip.

"That's because it was attacked by your mattress," I reply as I retrieve my clothes from her closet. My phone continues to ring as I get dressed. But I know that ringtone—it's my sister's, and the last thing I want to do right now is deal with her.

"Did you have fun?" I ask Cressida.

She chuckles. "Oh, yes. Having you, this big, scary, rich man, hide under my bed, was priceless." I grunt, to which she replies, "It was your choice to steal my key and break in."

"I didn't break in. I walked through the front door."

"Give me my key back," she demands, holding out her hand.

"No," I tell her with a smirk.

"If you break in again, especially while my son is here, I'll shoot you."

Her threat doesn't scare me. "You don't own a gun."

She offers me her coffee, and I take it as she walks to her closet. She makes a bit of noise before she steps back out, holding a small handgun, and points it at me.

"I'm impressed," I tell her.

"You want me to practice my shooting skills on

you? I'm sure they're better than my fork skills." She winks.

"I'll take your word for it." She lowers the gun to her side. "You know how to shoot?"

"Of course I do. I was raised on a farm," she scoffs.

"Are you actually any good, though?" I step closer to her.

"I bet I'm a better shot than you." She grins, and I can't help but lean down until our faces are only inches apart.

"I'd like to test that theory one day."

"I'm sure you would." She chuckles, then goes back to her closet and stores the gun in a safe I didn't notice before. She walks back out, takes the coffee from me, and waves a hand toward the door. "Goodbye, Soren. Don't come back."

"But you'll miss me too much if I don't come back," I tease.

"I will not, in fact, miss you too much. I won't miss you at all."

I move in and quickly steal a kiss, the split in my lip throbbing. Fuck, even with the hint of coffee lingering on her lips, she still tastes amazing. When I step back, her eyes are narrowed at me.

"Have a good day, Hurricane. I'll see you Monday at work."

She groans, and I step out of her house, closing the door slightly behind me. I flex my hand in the morning light, fingers curling slowly, tracing the faint puncture marks where Cressida's fork dug in. A small reminder of her edge, which has a small grin tugging at my mouth.

A voice cuts through the quiet. "Soren, right?" I turn to see her ex-husband standing just a few feet away. His posture is rigid, shoulders squared like he's bracing for a fight. His jaw is tight, lips pressed into a thin line, eyes narrow, sharp, and calculating, watching me like a predator sizing up prey.

No surprises here.

He's been waiting for this moment. Waiting to challenge me.

"Yes." My voice is steady, cold as steel.

He steps closer, eyes flashing. "You stayed the night with Cressida?" he asks.

"Yes," I say flatly, with no hesitation.

He studies me, searching for a crack. But I don't give him one. Inside, I'm already planning how to make it clear this isn't a fight he wants.

He nods and glances around. "Taylor has told me

about you. I don't know if I feel comfortable with a man like you around my son."

"I'm not planning to be around your son," I tell him, then add, "What does it matter who is fucking your ex, or did you forget, you got engaged and didn't even bother to tell the mother of your child?" I dig in a little further, because why the fuck not? I don't owe him any explanation.

"That's between us," he adds.

"And who she fucks is between us, at this current time," I throw back at him.

He just stares at me, and that's when I notice his car still sitting out at the curb.

He knew I was in there. *Interesting.*

"How did you know I was here?"

"It was a guess." That's all the explanation he gives before he turns away and goes back to his car.

THIRTY-ONE

CRESSIDA

On Monday morning, when I walk into the office, Soren's assistant informs me that he's in a meeting. She then shows me where my office is, which is conveniently located right near his. Pushing open the door, I spot a large box sitting on the desk.

"You have a meeting scheduled in an hour to get to know your staff. I'll come back and remind you." She leaves without another word, and I move over to the glass-topped desk with a black office chair behind it. I survey the box. It's closed, but the lid has my name written on it. I know I didn't order anything, so maybe this is something to do with work.

After pulling the lid off, I remove the packing material to find a vase. It's just like the one I threw at

Soren. But this one is a little larger and costs thousands more.

He bought me a new vase to replace the one I broke.

I'm not even sure how to feel about that.

Last night, while Oliver was eating spaghetti, I was searching online for another vase like the one I had. The only one I found was this one. However, it was too expensive, so I kept on looking. I could have bought a knockoff, and I considered it. Now I guess I don't have to worry about it. Smiling, I reach my hand in and lightly run my fingers over it.

"Now, if I could just get you to smile and touch me like that." I look up to find Soren leaning against the doorframe, watching me intently.

"You got me a new vase."

"I did. Do you approve?"

"I do. It's beautiful. Thank you," I tell him, and pull my hand back out.

Soren pushes off from the doorframe and comes to stand beside me. He lifts the box from my desk and places it on the floor. "I know something that's even more beautiful," he says, and I don't ask him what. "Are you ready to meet your staff?"

"What have you told them about me?" I ask,

opening my bag and pulling out my notepad and pen.

"They already know about you."

"How?"

"You may not be aware of this, but your name is actually quite well known in media land." He winks. "They are thrilled to be working with you, and know that you haven't been in this type of role for a while, but that you have experience with the job."

"Okay." I step from behind the desk, and his gaze scrolls over me. I can tell immediately he approves of what I'm wearing.

"You sure did a lot to stop a story," I comment.

"Hmm... Let's go."

For the rest of the day, Soren ushers me around and introduces me to everyone. At first, I'm greeted with a warm welcome, but I soon come to realize it's Soren who excites them. He must not personally show new employees around very often.

By the time we get back to my office, it's almost eleven. "Join me for lunch later?"

"No, that would look weird."

"You're a new employee. How would it look weird?"

"So, you have lunch with all your new employees?" I question.

"Never."

"Then, no." I wave him off. "Now, please leave so I can start the day."

He grins as he shuts the door.

I've been working in my office for a couple of hours when there's a knock on the door. I tell whoever it is to come in, and Layla pushes open the door with a bag in her hand. I can immediately smell the food, and it has my mouth watering.

"You shouldn't have. Thank you, Layla."

"It's from Mr. Nixon." She smiles as she places it on my desk.

I can't tell her to take it back to him, because that would make this situation weirder than it already is. Instead, I thank her again before she leaves.

I guess I could eat. But just as I open the bag and peek inside, my phone rings. It's a FaceTime call from Soren. I answer it, and his face comes into view.

"Do you like it?" he asks.

"Sure," I say and pull out a box of what smells like chicken.

"You didn't want to be seen eating lunch with me at work, and I respect that. So, we can do it this way." That's when I notice his lunch in front of him.

I chuckle. "You're *really* weird." I have to give him credit where credit is due, though. The lunch is nice. Especially when I take the first bite and remember I didn't eat breakfast this morning. I was so nervous about the staff not liking me for the sole reason that I came in and got a job that some of them had probably been trying to get. Then I have to remind myself I have been in the business for years, worked my way up, and I am good at what I do. *Why else would Soren have hired me?* You know, apart from trying to fuck me, and to stop me from writing the story about him. He is an astute businessman, after all. He could have put me anywhere. And, honestly, I think he's one of the smartest men I have ever met.

"Yes, and I'd like to be even weirder by sliding my hand up your skirt."

I can't tell if he's teasing or not.

But I laugh and then hang up on him.

THE REST of the workweek actually goes smoother than I thought it would. I hardly see Soren, which I'm thankful for because I don't want anyone to get any ideas that I only got the job because I am sleeping with the boss. Because let's be real, he gave me the job so I'd stop investigating him for the story.

That doesn't mean I'm going to stop digging, though, completely. Now that I know him better, I want to learn more about him.

I understand his life revolves around work and his sister, and that he's trying to set some boundaries with her because she's a fucking nutcase. And he understands that my life revolves around work and my son.

I texted Noah the other day to discuss me taking Oliver away next month to visit my family for a week. He asked if I could already get time off work, since I just started a new job. I told him it shouldn't be an issue, but truth be told, I haven't even checked.

I haven't seen Soren all day, but as I close my office door on my way out for the weekend, he steps out of his office at the same time. It's late, and no one else is in the office apart from a few stragglers. He sees me, and a small smile touches his lips. I want to say that my heart doesn't skip a beat at that barely-there smile, but it damn-well does.

I'm not really sure what he's doing to me, because it's so different from my last relationship. Not that I would call what we have a relationship. I just don't know what category to put us in. Yes, we've had sex. And, yes, we work together. But I don't know what else we are.

I manage to put one foot in front of the other and head down the hall, having to walk past his office to get to the elevator. He knows that, so he stands there, waiting for me. As soon as I reach him, I stop and meet his eyes.

"Care to have dinner with me?" he asks.

"I have Oliver tonight."

"Bring him," he says, and I give him a skeptical look. "I'm serious. Bring him. It's casual anyway."

"You're willingly inviting me, and my son, to dinner?"

"Yes, at my apartment," he adds.

"Umm... that's a lot."

"It's not. I have a chef, and you need to eat. So, come. What's his favorite food? I can get the chef to make it."

"I don't think that's a good idea."

"It is. Don't overthink it. Just come and have a glass of wine with me while we eat."

I should tell him no.

I don't bring my son around strange men.

But I guess I can introduce him as my boss?

Can't I?

That wouldn't be as weird.

"I'm telling him you're my boss."

"Whatever you need to do." He winks and heads

to the front of the office. I follow, and we ride in the elevator together. He pushes the button, and we stand in awkward silence as the car descends a few floors. Then, all of a sudden, his hand is sliding around my waist, and he's pushing me back against the wall, his body pressed against mine, his other hand cupping the back of my head.

And he kisses me.

He's kissing me.

In the elevator.

At work.

The elevator doesn't stop as we descend to the lobby. His tongue tangles with mine, and I drop my bag so I can wrap my fingers around the lapels of his suit jacket.

We have to stop doing this.

At least that's what I keep telling myself.

But it feels so fucking good.

And I don't think I can stop.

Just before the doors open, he pulls back and gives me a lust-filled look. "I'll see you later." He winks and strides out.

And I can only stand there, dazed.

The doors begin to shut, and I hurry out, catching my reflection in the shiny metal doors and seeing that my pink lipstick is smudged.

It was so worth it.

ONE OF THE highlights of my day is collecting Oliver from after-school care. I check my watch as I stand at the front and wait for him. He's usually always out first when he knows I will collect him. So, when the kids keep coming, and I see no sign of Oliver, I immediately go to where his class is. His teacher smiles when she sees me. "Oliver, have you seen him?" I ask her, looking around.

"He was the first out as usual. Is everything okay?" she says when the smile on my face drops at her words.

"He wasn't out there," I whisper. "I was only a few minutes late, but he wasn't out there," I manage to say again.

"Miss Knight, what about his dad? Did he collect him? It happens more often than not, the wrong parent comes, forgetting about their day." She laughs it off, but the pit in my stomach is dropping even lower.

Noah and I never get our days wrong.

It's something we are good at.

I press *call* anyway. Noah answers, and immediately I rush out, "Is Oliver with you?" He goes silent on his end.

"No."

My phone drops from my hand, and my heart starts racing faster and faster than ever before. I could not think of anything worse. Oliver would never have walked off without a parent or someone he knew. It's just not who he is. He knows the rules.

"Miss Knight, is everything okay?" I glance at her, a haze covering my eyes, and I realize it's getting blurry. "Miss Knight, who can I call?"

"911, I need to go to the police station. I need..." I collect my phone and run as fast as I can.

Where is Oliver?

THIRTY-TWO

SOREN

Why did I invite Cressida and her son to my house for dinner? At first, I considered her an annoyance. Somehow, she's worked her way into my life, into the parts of me I keep behind walls of steel. I'm not the type to focus on a woman like this. I don't do attachments. I don't have soft spots. And yet, here she is. It's not just lust or a passing convenience. It's quieter, deeper, something I'm not used to, something I don't know I can handle.

It isn't easy because I've never once focused on a woman the way I focus on her. I always thought doing so would hinder me and my career. Sure, I could fuck a woman, but that doesn't mean I'm going to give them anything more. Not that Cressida would ask for anything. She is definitely not the type for that. I had to argue with her just to get her to accept my job offer. So, I know it's not the money side of things that is keeping her around.

I check my watch again, noting that she's late.

The chef almost has dinner ready.

She said her son's favorite food is pizza, so I got the chef to make pizza, mac and cheese, salad, and some cupcakes, since I'm not sure what a kid eats. I had to Google it.

I try calling her, but she doesn't answer.

When I call a second time, it's her ex-husband who answers the phone. "She can't talk right now," he says with venom in his voice.

"Why not?"

"Because we're trying to find our fucking son," he growls, then hangs up.

What does he mean by that?

My phone rings, and I accept the call, not realizing it's Boston.

"Soren."

"Yes."

"We have an issue."

"What type of issue?" I ask.

"Cressida is at the police station, talking to an officer."

"Okay..." I reply, confused.

"Her son is missing." I clutch the edge of the countertop until my knuckles turn white. "It gets worse." He pauses. "I hacked the school's cameras, and nothing came up. So, I searched around the area, found a convenience store across the road with a camera, and asked to see their footage."

It's only been two hours since I left her. *How could this all happen in that time span?* I know she was going straight to the school to collect Oliver. He goes to an after-school program for working parents. I assumed she would pick him up and come straight here.

She didn't.

And now I know why.

"Look, I haven't shared it yet. But you might want to know."

"What?"

"It was Maya, Soren. Maya has him."

Jesus Christ! My heart drops into my stomach.

"What do you mean?"

"I mean, it's Maya I saw walking off with him. And I think you might have an hour or so before Cressida and her ex find out. This is a child, Soren. *Fix it.*" He hangs up.

I tell the chef to leave and that I will pay him for his time, and then I call my sister.

She doesn't answer.

Pulling up the tracker I have on her phone, I easily find her location.

I STOP the car outside the familiar house, our childhood home, which I had to sell after Dad died to pay off his debts. As soon as I had the money to do so, I bought it back. It's been sitting empty ever since. I gave Maya the keys to the place many years ago, and while I send someone around every three months to mow the lawns, I don't really do much else for it. The grass is currently overgrown, and the hedges need a really good trim.

I think I bought it for her so she could hold on to some good memories—what few there are. I figured she might want to live in it, but it turns out she likes the life of luxury a lot more.

I get out of the car, head up the path to the front door, and don't bother knocking, since I own the place, rage boiling up inside of me at what she has done. To the only woman I have ever cared about more than her. When I walk inside, I find Oliver sitting on the floor opposite my sister, and they are playing a game of *Monopoly*. They both turn to look at me. Maya smiles, and Oliver looks at me curiously, not knowing who I am or why I'm here.

"Your mother has been looking for you, Oliver. Please call her." I offer him my phone, and he gets up and takes it. He presses the call button on her contact, which reads 'Hurricane', and this time she answers straight away.

"Soren."

"Mom?" Oliver says.

"Oliver! Oh, my God. Are you okay? Where are you, and why are you with Soren?"

"This lady came to my school and said I needed to go with her to meet up with you and your boyfriend," he explains.

My gaze narrows at Maya, who sits there and smiles, like she's done nothing wrong. This is a new low, so fucking low of her. I try to contain my anger around Oliver, who clearly has no idea what has happened. Maya's eyes flick to me, and concern is there, but she can tell that I'm trying to contain my anger right now.

"Are you all right? Please tell me you're okay," she rushes out.

"Yes, I'm good. We had dinner and were playing a game. Can I come home now?"

"Yes. Yes. Please hand the phone back to Soren

for me so I can get the address." He looks up at me and hands me the phone.

"Hurricane."

"Don't you fucking 'Hurricane' me. It was your crazy-ass sister who took my son?" She waits a breath for me to answer.

"Yes."

"Where is he? Tell me *right now*."

"It's twenty minutes outside of the city. I'll send you the address."

"I'm already in Noah's car. We're on our way," she says and hangs up.

I shake my head at Maya.

"Do you play games?" Oliver asks me.

I look down at him and see an innocent boy, having no idea what just happened. "Not really," I answer him truthfully.

"So, what do you do for fun?" he asks.

I glance at Maya to see her watching us. She bites her lip as she watches, and I look back down at him.

"I practice boxing." I think that's better than saying I like the rush of making others bleed by my hands.

"Can you teach me how to fight? The boys are mean at my school," he chirps up at his words.

"He's really good," Maya chimes in.

My eyes narrow at her before I look back to Oliver. "Oliver, could you please go see if the light works in that back room?" I point, he nods, and he goes to check it out.

Once he's gone, I squat down so I'm eye-level with Maya. The house might be in a nice neighborhood, but inside it's a different story. The floors are dull and sticky underfoot, the kind of grime that only comes from months of neglect. Dust clings to the furniture, and the air carries a faint musty dampness that makes me wonder if there's mold creeping behind the wallpaper. The carpet has seen better days—matted, stained, and far from what it once was. Every corner whispers of wasted money and lost pride.

"What have you done?" I ask her.

"You can't start a new family without me, Soren," she answers.

I take a slow breath, steadying myself.

"You just ended ours."

THIRTY-THREE

Cressida

Noah drives as fast as possible, and I'm thankful for that. He's been fuming the whole way, and hasn't said a word to me.

When I arrived at his school and was told Oliver wasn't there, I called Noah, thinking he had him.

I was wrong.

I panicked.

This is a mother's worst fear.

I searched the school, screaming his name.

The police were called and asked us to come down to report the case.

And then Soren called when we were out searching again.

My hands haven't stopped shaking since I learned Oliver was missing.

Soren's car is parked out front of a house, and before Noah even stops the car, I'm already running through the overgrown lawn and straight to the front door. Rushing inside, I find Oliver sitting on the floor with Soren, laughing at something he said.

Oliver turns, and his eyes find mine. "Mom!" he yells and jumps up to hug me. Bending down, I squeeze his little body tightly until I hear footsteps behind me.

"Hey, buddy, you had us worried," Noah says with false calm, and Oliver goes to him and wraps his little arms around Noah's waist.

Soren stands, brushing the dirt from his trousers. I can't help it when my eyes narrow at him. "Noah, please take Oliver to the car. I need to speak with Soren alone."

Noah glances at Soren with a nod, then says, "Thanks for finding him," and walks out with his arm around Oliver's shoulders.

Taking a steadying breath, I turn my attention back to Soren. "Where is she?" I ask, my hands balled at my sides.

He jerks a thumb over his shoulder, indicating another room. I storm past him and into the kitchen, where I find Maya leaning over the counter, playing on her phone as if nothing has happened. She raises her head when she hears me enter. There is no remorse evident in her eyes at all.

"Don't look so mad. You got him back," she says and almost laughs, like this was all some big joke.

I sense Soren behind me, but I can't think straight. Anger is the only thing that's fueling me right now. So, I bend down to remove one of my high heels, and then I move so quickly that she doesn't have time to react before I slam the heel down straight into her hand. Her screams rip through the air, and I lean in close. "I should do worse, but my son is in the car. If I see you again, especially around my child, there will be no stopping me." I slip the heel back on my foot and turn around to find both Noah and Soren watching me.

"We need to go," I tell Noah.

Soren doesn't say a word as I walk past him, brushing shoulders as I leave him there with his sobbing psycho of a sister.

Bitch deserved what she got and more.

"You're kind of a badass," Noah says with a laugh.

"I'll do anything to protect our son," I tell him.

"We know," he says as we approach the car where Oliver is waiting for us. "Soren stopped me from stepping in and keeping you from hurting her. He said, 'Let her,' so I stood there as you smashed her hand."

I take in his words.

Soren let me hurt his sister.

The one person who is *everything* to him.

I climb into the back seat with Oliver, and I don't look back as we drive off.

Soren doesn't come into work the following week, and I don't hear from him or see him at all.

The following Monday, he arrives and heads straight into his office, not speaking one word to me. Not that I expected him to, but part of me hoped he would at least acknowledge me, considering the reason I was in that situation in the first place was because of him and his crazy-ass sister.

"Miss Knight, Mr. Nixon is asking for a meeting with you."

"Thank you, Layla." I head to his office, and he looks up as I enter.

"Shut the door, please," he says.

I do, and when I turn around, he's watching me warily. I take a seat and wait for him to tell me what this meeting is about.

"You've requested time off," he states.

"I did."

"It's approved. You can leave now." He just stares at me after making that announcement and says nothing more. So, I stand, unsure of what's happening. I go to the door, and as I grip the handle, I glance back at him.

His gaze is still locked on me.

"Where is your sister?" I ask.

"In the hospital," he tells me.

I want to ask if everything is okay, but I don't because I don't care about her *at all*.

Fuck her!

Though I can't deny his appearance clearly indicates he's fighting his own demons: his hair is unkempt, as if he has been running his hands through it too many times, and he has dark circles under his eyes.

Nodding once, I open the door and walk out.

Layla eyes me curiously but doesn't say anything.

I thought I would miss my old job, but it turns out I really enjoy what I'm doing here. When I don't have Oliver, I'm usually the first to arrive and the last to leave. Today, though, I have to leave early because I'm picking up Oliver, and I promised to take him for ice cream.

He's mentioned Soren a few times. He said he likes him. I've brushed it off every time because I didn't expect them to meet the way they did, and that Oliver would take to Soren the way he has. Thankfully, Oliver doesn't understand what has been happening because the crazy-ass bitch didn't tell him anything. Thank fuck for small mercies at least.

I collect my things, and on my way out, I glance into Soren's office. He's sitting at his desk, his head in his hands, looking like he's contemplating life. A part of me wants to go in there and check if he's okay. All the other parts know better, and they keep my feet moving toward the exit.

If he really cared, he would have called me by now. But I don't think he does. It was all because I was a woman who was there and available.

The next few days pass quickly, and when I pick Oliver up from school on Wednesday, like always, he tells me all about his day. I smile at him, and once again, like always, I wonder how I got so lucky when it comes to my son. I briefly considered having more children, but soon concluded one was enough for me. Noah always wanted more kids, and I guess he can do that now with his new fiancée.

They sent me an invitation to their wedding. I don't think it's appropriate for me to go, even if I still get along with him and his family. It's a new beginning for him, and I don't want to be there to taint it with old memories of us. We will always remain connected because of Oliver, but I don't think we should go any further than that.

When we arrive back at my place, Noah is already waiting for us. We agreed that he could have him tonight since I plan on leaving on Saturday to spend a week at my family's house.

"Hey, buddy," Noah says, patting Oliver's shoulder. "Go get your things." Oliver runs inside, and I turn to face Noah as we wait.

"I got the wedding invite. I won't be there, Noah."

"I figured as much, but I thought I would ask." I nod as I glance at the door. "Bet your family is excited," I say, turning back to him with a small smile.

"They are. They already have it all planned out." He chuckles. "Be prepared for Oliver to come back a horse rider."

I laugh.

"Oh, yes, I remember when they tried to get me on a horse. Didn't end well."

"Well, lucky for you, Oliver has more coordination." He clears his throat, then asks, "Have you spoken to him?"

"Who?"

"Soren."

"Not since the other day when he approved my leave." He nods and tucks his hands into his pockets.

"He's a very peculiar man," he notes.

"He is," I agree.

"Have you heard anything more about his sister?"

"Only that she's in the hospital, which is less than she deserves."

I smile as Oliver runs out, carrying his backpack. I lean down and kiss his cheek. "Have the best time. I'll see you tomorrow. We'll go on a plane to see the family." He loves flying but doesn't get to do it often.

"I can't wait. Love you, Mom. Bye." I wave as I watch them drive away.

Going back inside, I see a notification on my phone for a fight tonight. I signed up for these notifications when I was first investigating Soren, but I only requested to be notified when he was fighting.

I quickly change out of my work clothes, opting

for a pair of jeans, a loose top, and some flats. I keep my hair up in its high bun and don't bother touching up my makeup. I'm already running late, so I grab my bag and run out the door.

He seems to be avoiding me, and I want to see him. I have no intention of talking to him, though. What his sister did was so wrong, and I hate that small part of me that still blames him, even in the slightest. I enjoy watching him fight. I've only been to a few of his fights, and they're actually fucking hot to witness.

The ride to the old warehouse doesn't take too long, and I'm soon climbing out of the Uber and heading inside. There's already a fight going on as I push my way through the crowd, but it's not Soren in the ring.

The announcer yells, "Knockout!" and I know the next fight will start soon.

I take a spot in the middle of the crowd, close enough to see but hopefully not close enough for Soren to notice me. The crowd starts to cheer, and I know he's heading out for his turn in the ring.

When I catch a glimpse of him, I note his head is tilted down as he slowly strides to the middle of the ring. His opponent watches him with a little bit of caution. I don't blame him. Soren's hands are fucking lethal.

The bell rings, and the fight starts, but it's not like the other times I've seen Soren fight. Something is different. It's as if he doesn't want to be here, which is weird because this is his happy place.

The sound of a fist meeting flesh echoes through the crowd, and everyone gasps loudly. Hands meeting face, in the most brutal way possible.

Another punch.

This one to his stomach.

Soren is standing there, letting himself get pummeled. He doesn't move, just takes hit after hit. The other fighter stares at Soren in confusion, because usually Soren's opponents would be on the ground by now. But here he is, still standing, and taking it all.

"Soren!" I scream, pushing through the thickening crowd, every second stretching tight with panic. My eyes lock onto him just a few feet away, unaware. When I'm closer to the ring, I scream his name again, until my own ears are ringing. His head snaps toward me, sharp and alert. For a brief moment, it feels like he might catch the danger. And then a sudden, brutal blow strikes his temple. He crumples instantly, the world tilting as he hits the ground.

THIRTY-FOUR

SOREN

My head is throbbing.

I brought it upon myself.

I shouldn't have been out there tonight.

But I needed to feel something.

It was the best option for me.

Because that night when Cressida left me at my childhood home, Maya had to be admitted to the hospital for her heart. It's always been bad, and at one stage, we assumed she was getting better, but she has always had heart problems, plus mental health issues. Thankfully, she's doing better now, but it's really fucking hard to try to walk away from someone who only has you. But she's losing her fucking mind, and I don't want Cressida to be caught up in all that bullshit.

Hands wrap around my upper arms and lift me from where I'm sprawled on the ground. It's clear I've lost the fight, which isn't surprising. It's the first fight I've lost in a very long time, and it doesn't feel good.

My vision is blurry, but my gaze seeks her out, only to find her behind me with a worried expression on her face. I feel the stares of the people in the crowd, and I know she can too. I ask her with nothing more than a look to come with me to the locker room, and she thankfully understands, indicating that she'll follow.

We push past the crowd and straight into the locker room. When the door is shut, separating us from the noise in the main room, I slump onto the bench in front of my locker. My head still feels light and fuzzy.

She remains by the door, not coming too close to me.

"Why are you here?" I ask.

Ignoring my question, she asks one of her own, "Why did you let him win?"

Fuck, even with my vision fucked up like it is, I can still see she's the most beautiful woman I have ever laid eyes on.

Dropping my head between my knees, I take a

few deep breaths. My ribs are sore, possibly bruised or broken. My head is pounding from the beating I let him give me, but it made me feel things. That's why I let him do it.

"You should see a doctor," she says.

"I know what he'll say." I sit up.

"Fine, if you won't see a doctor, then I'll look after you. Where are your keys?"

"You can't drive," I remind her.

"Of course I can. I just don't like driving in the city." She digs into my bag and pulls out my keys. "Get up. We need to get ice on your injuries."

"Why are you here?" I ask again. "You hate me."

"I don't hate you. I hate your sister."

She takes my bag and lifts it over her shoulder.

"I don't need your help," I mumble.

"You do. Do you want the pain? Do you need more of it? I can stab you again if that's what you're after," she says, and a small smile plays on my lips, which hurts because I was punched in the mouth.

"No. I know you have marvelous stabbing abilities, but I would rather not be on the receiving end of that again."

She shrugs and starts for the back door when all of a sudden, the other door opens, and Arlo and Reon walk in. Of course, tonight is the night both of them decide to come. They immediately notice Cressida.

Arlo waggles his brows before he turns to me. "So, this is where you've been hiding," Arlo says. "With the reporter."

Reon eyes Cressida with a bit of contempt, and I know he's judging her. "You're seeing a reporter?" Reon asks.

"No," Cressida answers. "And not that it's any of your business, but I used to be a journalist. Get it right!" She rolls her eyes, then adds, "Good to see you both again."

To me, she says, "I'll wait for you in your car." And then she leaves.

The last time she saw Arlo was at the awards gala I took her to. Before that, she saw both of them at a party she crashed to get more information on me for her story. Neither of them nor their partners gave her anything, but I have to give her credit where credit is due because she tried hard.

"You took a beating," Arlo notes.

"Maya is out of the hospital," Reon says.

"I did. And, yes, I know." I sigh. "Why are you here?"

"We were concerned. You missed the last party,

and you haven't been active recently. You are our Lord, or did you forget that?" Arlo explains.

"I was at the hunt," I remind them. "But you're right. I am your Lord, and it would do you both well to remember that."

"Or what? You'll let us beat you?" Reon scoffs, clenching his fists. "I see that's what you seem to enjoy these days."

"Yeah, well, maybe today I did."

"You should stop fighting here. If you want to be beaten, come to me. I'll happily break a few of your ribs," Reon offers with a glint in his eye.

"Of course you would."

I glance at the back door.

"Getting into a relationship with a woman who was trying to take you down is not ideal," Arlo says, always trying to be the voice of reason.

"I'm not in a relationship with her," I tell him, voice clipped and cool. Not yet. Not like I want to be. I hate that I have to say it like this, like it's a fact I'm trying to convince myself of as much as him. *Because if I'm honest, none of this is simple.*

"Now, if that's all, I need to leave." I turn away before I say something I can't take back.

"My wife would like you to come to our wedding anniversary party," Reon says. "Two years," he adds proudly. "Though I can't guarantee she won't try to kill you."

"She's wanted to kill me for many years now."

"That she has."

With nothing left to say, I head out the back door, leaving them standing in the dressing room.

THIRTY-FIVE

Case Notes

Do not cook for the enemy.

I'M SITTING in his car, waiting.

It doesn't take long before I see him emerge from the building, one arm wrapped around his ribs like he's holding himself together. They're probably killing him, though I doubt he'd ever admit it.

Soren slides into the passenger seat with a wince he tries to hide, turns his head toward me, and smirks. "If your plan is to kill me with your driving, I just want you to know, I'm fully prepared to die with you."

I scoff as I start the car. "I would never kill myself. I have my son to think about."

"Good to know." After a beat, he adds, "He seems like a good kid."

"He is." I hesitate before confiding, "He liked you." When he doesn't reply right away, I glance at him to find him staring out the window.

"Kids don't like me," he finally says.

"My kid did."

We drive in silence for a few minutes, and I wonder what it is that broke this man so much.

"Your friends... They don't like you hanging out with me, do they?"

"Who cares what they think?" he replies, then asks, "What do you plan to do once you get me home?"

"Oliver is with his father tonight, so I'll stay with you to make sure you don't die. You could have a concussion."

"I don't."

"So what? You're a doctor now?"

"No." He points up ahead and says, "Turn right just up there."

I do as he says, and we're pulling into his parking

lot. He tells me where to park, and I drive into the spot. I grab his bag from the back seat, then get out of the car, meeting him near the trunk.

I wasn't planning on staying here with him, but I don't want him to be alone if something happens and he needs someone. We step into the elevator, and I make sure there is plenty of space between us, not wanting a repeat of what happened in the elevator at work.

I'm pretty sure that if I let him put his hands on me, I'd give in to almost anything he wants. And I can't have that happening again. Last time I let my guard down, my son being kidnapped was the result.

When we reach his condo, I follow him inside. I place his gym bag on the kitchen counter as he grabs some aspirin for his head. I watch him swallow the pills with a drink of water.

He's still shirtless, since he didn't bother showering or changing before we left the warehouse, and I can see that his torso is turning different colors of purple and blue from where he let the guy hit him. His face has dried blood on it, and his eye is starting to swell.

Why did he let that guy beat him like this?

I understand that Soren likes fighting and that

he's good at it, but he didn't even fight back. He just stood there and took the hits like a fucking fool.

"You're mad," he says.

"Yes. Why would you do that?" I ask, waving a hand at his face. "What will your colleagues say?"

"I don't care." He shrugs, groaning in pain at the movement.

"You need to shower. Have you eaten?"

"No."

"I'll make something. *Go.*" I shoo him off.

Opening the refrigerator, I see leftover pizza that looks inedible, so I throw it out and grab some pasta and frozen fried chicken. After tossing the chicken into the air fryer to reheat it, I prepare the pasta to place underneath it. When everything is almost done, he walks into the kitchen in nothing but a pair of boxers, appearing tired but clean. And still hot as hell, despite his injuries.

I hate that I like the way he looks.

"It smells good," he says as I pull the chicken out.

"I cooked whatever you had," I tell him. "You had leftover pizza in the fridge, but I threw it out."

"That was from the night I invited you and Oliver over."

I can't reply because that goes down as one of the

most terrifying nights of my life. It's not a night I wish to relive. Oliver is safe now, and I will ensure he stays that way because I will never let *her* get near him *ever* again.

"As you probably already know from your research into me, Maya and I didn't have the greatest upbringing. She was a sick teenager with a drunk father who had gambling issues and used all our money, and I had to step up. I was put in a lot of debt from her medical bills, and before I knew it, I was fighting to make money."

"I'm sorry about that, but I can't find it in me to have compassion for her," I tell him honestly.

"I'm not asking you to. I want to explain to you why I have protected Maya for so long."

"Was it protection? Is that the word you would use?" I ask as I slide his food over the counter to him, then get him a bottle of water from the refrigerator.

"Yes, that's how I saw it."

"Okay."

"You disagree?"

"I do. I think you felt guilty, and that led to you enabling Maya's bad behavior."

"I would never encourage what she did," he insists.

"Maybe not knowingly. Do you still give her money?"

"I stopped."

"When?"

"The week before..." He trails off, and I fit the pieces together.

"She thinks it's *my fault* that you cut her off. So, her payback was to make *me* hurt. Probably in the hopes that I would be so angry that I would never want to see you again," I tell him.

"She doesn't know what's happening between us. I don't even know. Do you?" he asks, searching my eyes for an answer I don't have.

"*Nothing* is happening between us." The words come out sharp, too quickly. Truth is, I don't know what's happening either. Maybe I'm scared to admit it. Or maybe I'm just confused.

So, why am I here? The question echoes inside me, louder than I want it to. Because part of me can't stop wanting him, wants whatever this is, even if it's a mess.

"So, why are you here, then?"

Touché, motherfucker.

"You are my boss, and I wanted to make sure you're okay."

"Why did you come to the fight?"

I grab a fork from the drawer. "I like watching you fight."

"Your son asked me to train him," he says nonchalantly.

"Sorry, what?"

"When he asked me what I do for fun, I told him I box. He asked me if I could teach him because kids are mean to him at school."

I stand there, baffled at this information. Oliver has never mentioned to me that he's being bullied, and yet he told a man he hardly knows.

"Do you plan to stab me again?" he asks, and I notice I'm holding the fork a little too tightly.

"He's being bullied?" I ask as I hand over the fork.

"I don't think so. I asked him about it, and he just mentioned that kids are mean."

That makes me sad. You never want your kid to feel like an outsider or an easy mark for someone to pick on.

"He's a good kid, and I would be happy to train him."

"Thank you." I rest my elbows on the counter and stare at him as he eats.

"Are you eating?" he questions.

"I've eaten already. Plus, I have to make sure you don't die on me."

"You leave in a few days for your trip, right?" he asks, changing the subject.

"Yep. I'm so excited to see my family. I feel like it's been forever since I hugged my mother."

His expression shifts to something like confusion at my confession, and I smile at him as he continues to eat.

"Are you giving Maya money again?" I ask.

"No."

"Are you telling me the truth?"

"Lying to you seems almost impossible now," he says and takes another bite.

"Tell me about the Forsaken."

He groans, and I know it's not something he can talk about, but I thought I would try.

"How does it feel to be the Lord?"

"How do you even know that word?" he asks.

"I've learned a lot. Want to know what?" I smirk as I eagerly wait for him to answer.

"Tell me."

"Are you sure? I mean, you aren't going to kill me or anything?"

"I won't kill you."

"Okay, good. So, what I have learned is that you

have different types of events for your members. For example, one is for girlfriends or boyfriends, and no wives are allowed." I watch him intently, but he gives nothing away, so I continue, "The other is for wives, though one of your members, Reon, had his wife at an event that was for girlfriends only."

"They are inseparable." He lets this tidbit slip, and I nod.

"He seems to really love her."

"Yes, they are in love," he confirms.

"And then we have the hunts."

He noticeably tenses at my words, and I know I've hit something big. I never intended to bring this up to him. I thought I would let my work die when I started working for him. It was probably one of the most complex stories I've ever worked on. Getting information about the Forsaken is almost impossible, and what I have is only hearsay. I never had any proof. They've obviously been a tight-lipped group for many years. I don't even know precisely how long the Society has been around.

"I don't know how often the hunts happen, or when they happen, but stories have been whispered that it's not animals you hunt."

He remains silent as he sits across from me, waiting for me to talk again. But that's all the information I have. I know he's some leader in the Society, which makes sense because he's a mighty powerful man. Not that the other members aren't powerful in their own right, but he is on a different level. I'm not really sure how to explain it.

"I'm getting tired," he admits, then yawns.

"Good. Let's go watch a movie," I suggest.

"I don't watch movies."

"You have to. No sleeping," I admonish as I put his plate in the sink.

Soren's phone starts ringing, and we both see Maya's name flash on the screen.

"If she comes here, I am not going to be held responsible for what I do to her," I warn him.

"She doesn't have keys any longer," he says. "What movie are we going to watch?"

"*Pride and Prejudice.*" I smile happily.

"That sounds like an awfully boring movie."

"Shut up. It's based on one of the *best* romance books ever written." I exaggerate a swoon as I kick off my shoes and fall back onto his large sofa. I tap the spot next to me, and he comes over and sits. He smells of vanilla and whatever else is in his body wash.

"I prefer a movie where everyone dies," he grumbles.

"How boring," I reply.

I find the movie on a streaming platform and press *play*.

As the opening credits roll, I turn to find him staring at me.

THIRTY-SIX

SOREN

How do I keep her here and never let her escape?

If I could fill this place with her things, her scent, her laughter, I'd do it in a heartbeat.

I want her here full-time.

The idea hits harder than I expected. *What does that even mean?* That after years of convincing myself I don't need a relationship, that I don't want a wife... Maybe I do?

Wife. Where the fuck did that thought come from?

I'm not paying attention to the movie. My gaze is locked on her profile as she smiles brightly at the screen, her raven-black hair still in the bun she wore to work. Her legs are folded under her ass as she reclines on the couch, leaning on a pillow.

"You *can* watch the movie, you know," she tells me, fully aware that my focus is on her.

"I'd rather be watching you." And I'm not lying. She is way more interesting than what is happening on the stupid television.

"Don't make this harder than it already is, Soren."

"What's hard?" I ask.

She waves a finger between us. "*Us*. We can *never* be together. I don't know if I will ever feel safe having my son with anyone but his father again, and that's thanks to your sister."

I adjust my position slightly and feel the burn in my ribs. They probably aren't broken, but for sure bruised, which is fine. I've dealt with worse than this.

"So, we're friends?" I ask.

"Have you ever been friends with someone you've fucked?" Her gaze flicks between me and the movie she seems to love so much.

"Can't say that I have."

"Yeah, I didn't think so. Look..." She takes a deep breath, and for a split second, something flickers in her eyes: hesitation, maybe regret. Her tone softens, just barely, like she's fighting to keep control. "I can find another job. We can end whatever this is, and have a clean break."

"That's what you want?"

"I think it's for the best, don't you?" Her voice is steady, but there's a slight catch in the way she says it, just enough to make me pause. Like maybe she's asking the question more for herself than for me.

"It's not me offering it," I remind her.

"Well, then, yes. I think it's for the best." She glances away, her voice a little quieter. "I'll stay a few more hours, then I have to go. I need to pack for my trip."

"You can keep your job, Cressida." I can see her pulling away, and it tugs on something deep inside of me. The last thing I want is for her to pull away from me.

She blinks, frozen, and then blinks again. "You rarely call me by my name."

"You're my employee, so I should be using your name."

"I guess you're right."

She turns back to the television, and we stay like that until the movie is finished. Her watching the movie. Me watching her. She doesn't look my way again, even though I know she knows I'm staring at her. She doesn't comment on it again either.

When I sense she's about to leave, I stand at

almost the same time she does, ignoring the pull at my ribs.

"Thank you, Soren," she says.

"For what?"

"I guess for not killing me." She smirks, then she turns and heads for the door.

I want to tell her to stop, to come back. Beg her to stay so we can work through this. And while I have always been a selfish man, something about her makes me not want to be with her. The last thing I want to do is cause her more pain. I've already done enough of that.

THIRTY-SEVEN
CRESSIDA

THE TIME OLIVER and I spend with my family is really good, but I miss home. I haven't heard from Soren since I left. I didn't think I would, but you know, there's always that little devil on your shoulder that whispers to you.

Mine needs to shut up.

I'm sitting at the firepit when Izzy approaches. Her daughter is currently running around chasing chickens while Oliver chases her. It's so cute.

"How is Noah?" she asks.

My other sister, Anna, sits on the opposite side of the fire, holding a glass of wine. Their husbands are inside watching a game as our father is preparing food. Our mother comes over with two glasses and passes me one before she takes the seat next to me.

"He's doing well. He sent me an invite to his wedding. I told him I regretfully decline."

"And how is Soren?" Izzy asks, smiling behind her glass of wine.

"Soren? Who is that?" my mother asks.

"Google Soren Nixon," Izzy tells Anna. And Anna immediately grabs her phone. I know the second she gets to a photograph of him because her eyes go wide, and she stares up at me. Her gaze flicks to Izzy, who nods in confirmation before she looks back at me.

"Who is that man?" Anna asks with a sly grin.

"He's Cres's new friend," Izzy unhelpfully says.

"He's my boss," I correct.

Anna hands the phone to our mother, who raises her brows when she sees the image.

"You like this man?" Mom questions.

"No."

"Now, Cressida, you know not to lie to your mother," Mom chides.

I look over to where Oliver is and let out a sigh. "I do, but I can't be with him."

"Why?" Izzy asks.

"I haven't told you what happened."

"What happened?" Mom prods.

I'm sitting with the three most important women

in my life. I heave out a breath because I know they're going to kill me for not telling them before now. But everything happened so fast that night, and afterward, I didn't want to think about it anymore. Didn't want to relive the panic clawing at my chest or the silence that followed when I realized he was gone.

"I went to pick up Oliver from the after-school program, like I usually do when I have to work late, but when I got to the school, he wasn't there."

My mom puts her hand over her heart, and her gaze searches for Oliver before she lets out a relieved breath. That small motion, the way her shoulders drop, and the tremor in her exhale nearly undoes me.

My voice is shaking, but I stay put together as I continue, "Soren's sister hates me. She believes I'm the reason Soren cut her off financially. So, she decided the best form of payback was to take Oliver."

The words taste bitter. Saying them out loud makes it all real again. The helplessness, the fear, the rage that I might never see my son's face again. I grip my knees to keep myself from breaking.

"She what?" Anna screams.

I wave a hand at her to calm down. "Soren found her, thankfully. And then I stabbed her hand with my heel. She didn't hurt Oliver, thank God. Her intention was purely to hurt me."

"That *evil* bitch," Anna growls. "Maybe I'll bring my whip with me next time I visit you, and have some practice with her head." She smiles, and despite myself, I can't help but smile back. I miss being surrounded by women who do nothing but love me. I'm pretty isolated where I am, but it's more by choice. I have very few friends in the city because I can work odd hours, and by the time I'm finally home, I want to spend some one-on-one time with my son.

"And this man...?" my mother asks.

"Soren."

"He found him?"

"He did. Then told me where they were."

"He looks at her as if she's the only woman in the room," Izzy gushes.

"Izzy, you aren't supposed to like him." I shake my head.

"What? I can't help it. I loved the way he looked at you. He didn't even notice I was sitting there." She smiles. "You want a man who only has eyes for you, right?"

"We ended whatever was building between us,

and agreed to just be friends," I tell them, and they give me disbelieving looks.

Oliver runs over and straight into my mother's lap, and she hugs him hard to her chest.

"Do you like Soren?" my mother asks Oliver.

"Yes! He's going to teach me how to box," he replies.

Once again, they're all staring at me.

"Oliver, why does Soren need to teach you that?" Mom inquires.

He plays with the end of his shirt, avoiding looking at me, then admits, "Timothy keeps pushing me, and he tells me I'm weak."

"You want to learn to defend yourself," my mother says, brushing her hand down his back, comforting him.

"Yes. And Soren is one of the best fighters."

"Who told you that?" I ask him.

"His sister," he says, and I cringe. "Can he teach me, Mom? I really want to learn to box."

"I'll think about it. Soren is a busy man."

"He said he would do it. I asked him."

"All right, I'll talk to him." He beams and runs over to kiss me before taking off again to chase chickens.

I'm not sure I'm making the right decision, but it

can't hurt to teach your child how to defend himself. Right?

"How is the rest of Soren's family?" Mom asks. "You mentioned the sister, but what about the rest?"

"They're dead."

"So, they are all each other has?"

"Yes."

"And he's cut ties with her?"

"He said he has."

"Hmm..." The three of them share a glance.

"What?" I ask.

"It seems like he did that for you," Mom says.

"He hasn't. And that crazy way of thinking is what allowed her to take Oliver in the first place," I say, more sternly than I'd intended.

"No one is blaming you. I think maybe you made that man see his mistakes. Maybe he's trying," she says.

"Sure," I say, standing, and then I remember that conversation I had with him about his sister.

"Good. Why don't you focus on that and leave me alone? She thinks I'm the reason for your sudden change of heart when it comes to her."

"You are." His voice is steady. Certain. There's no softness, just a fact laid bare.

My head jerks back in surprise. "What?"

"You are the reason. I realized it because of you."

I try not to dwell on those words or what my family said as I head inside to find my father in the kitchen cooking. My mother is the baker of the family, and my father is the cook.

My parents have a fantastic marriage. They've been together for more than forty years. Not once have I seen them fight to the point of no return. Yes, they argue now and then, which is healthy for a relationship, but my father is always the first to apologize.

I remember him sneaking up behind her, wrapping his arms around her waist, and telling her he loves her. The bad news is that I thought I had found that with Noah, but I was wrong. I don't regret that relationship for a single second, though, because it gave me Oliver.

"What's up, kiddo?" Dad asks.

"Just came in to see what you're doing."

"Or are you avoiding your mother and sisters?" He laughs and waves for me to come closer.

I always love helping him in the kitchen. My sisters hate it, and to this day, they still don't cook. I learned how to cook from my father. I'm not the greatest at it, but he taught me a few things for which I am grateful.

"You know, you're more like me than they are." He chuckles. "It's why I cook. It gives me a break from being surrounded by beautiful, opinionated women. However, I do miss having you around, kid. No one joins me in the kitchen anymore."

He hands me a peeler to start on the potatoes, then says, "Oliver is so big now. I miss seeing him."

"I'll try to bring him home more often," I tell him. "My life is just so busy. And I know that's not an excuse."

"Of course it is. You're a single woman in a city, raising a son. Life is busy." His words provide me with some comforting relief. "Though I would like to come visit you. We now have help on the farm since I'm getting older."

I stop peeling and look at him. "Really?"

"Yes, if that's okay with you."

"I would love that."

"So would I, kid. So would I."

THIRTY-EIGHT

SOREN

Cʀᴇssɪᴅᴀ ɪs ʙᴀᴄᴋ from her trip, but I haven't seen her. Though I have stalked her social media and seen many photographs of her and her family from the time she was away, I still don't know her well. She looks happy in almost every single one of them. A part of me is jealous that I can't make her that happy. I've tried to avoid listening to her conversations, because if she finds out, she'll probably kill me. Pretty sure I'd die with a smile on my face if it were she who killed me, though.

I spot Lilith and Reon as soon as I walk into their anniversary party. They don't have many guests, seeing as it is only a small gathering. Quite a few of the attendees are members of the Forsaken, and others are people Reon works with. I see a few women I don't recognize, and I'm guessing they're Lilith's friends.

I pause in my perusal of the room when I see Cressida, shocked, because I didn't even think I would be seeing her. She's dressed in all black, matching the color of her hair, and she's holding a glass of champagne. She looks gorgeous, effortlessly so. The soft lighting glints off the rim of her glass, catching the curve of her lips as she takes a slow sip. My chest tightens, and I can't look away.

Reon says my name, and I reluctantly drag my gaze from Cressida to find him and Lilith standing there.

"Oh, I see you recognize one of my guests," Lilith says.

I know she and Cressida have met before, but I didn't realize they were close enough for her to invite Cressida to parties. But then again, Lilith probably did it on purpose, thinking it would be payback. I don't think she will ever let me live down the torment I caused her. I don't blame her, but at the same time, I would do anything to protect the Society.

"You're good friends with Cressida, are you?" I ask her.

"No, I was just hoping to annoy you," she replies

cheerily, and I look at Reon to see him watching me. Lilith smiles and walks off, leaving us standing there.

"Your wife sure knows how to hold a damn grudge," I inform him.

"I know, it's one of my favorite things about her," he says with pride as I scan the room for Cressida again.

"She doesn't know you're in love with Cressida," he adds after a moment, and I spin to face him.

"Love?" I laugh, and he holds his face in a neutral expression. "Love?" I scoff.

"You offer to help train all the kids now? You don't seem like that type of guy, Soren," Reon says.

"Love?" I say again, confused with the words. Is he right that I wouldn't offer anyone training, yet I did it so easily for her and her child? And dare I say, I like the kid. "How the fuck do you know about that?" I throw back at him

"Yes, love. And I have my sources." He pats my back and then walks off, saying over his shoulder, "Be on your best behavior."

Of course, I'm going to be on my best behavior. I always am at these types of events. But I linger like a fucking stalker, watching Cressida, waiting for her to look my way, but she doesn't. Her back is to me, and

I can't help but note how her dress clings to her curves.

Arlo eventually comes up beside me, chuckling.

"Who would have thought you would be afraid of a woman?" he comments.

"I'm not."

"So, why haven't you gone over there yet?"

"I will when she's free."

"Yeah, you keep telling yourself that."

He leaves me and heads straight to where Cressida is talking to Cora. Arlo says something, then pulls Cora away, leaving Hurricane, my infuriating journalist, standing by herself. She turns, scanning the room, and then her gaze snags on mine. I'm leaning against a table, watching her. Our eyes lock, and it's like the rest of the room fades out, and there is just her standing there in that sexy as-sin black dress, looking at me like she is not sure whether to approach or run.

I don't miss the way her grip tightens around her champagne glass just before she takes a hesitant step in my direction. That single movement does something to me, something sharp and unwanted.

My heart rate picks up, and I think back to what Reon said.

Love.

Surely, that's not what this is.

I don't love her, do I?

It's just infatuation.

A pull I can't explain. A craving that won't burn out.

So, when does it go away?

One minute I want her to be my damn wife, and the next I'm ready to walk out before she gets the chance to hurt me. It's a war raging inside my chest with need fighting logic and heart against reason, and I don't know which side is winning anymore.

"Soren," she greets when she reaches me.

"Cressida." She flinches at the use of her name. "You look lovely," I tell her.

Her gaze pans over me, and she smiles. "Thank you, as do you." She nods.

Small talk.

Yep, we can do that.

"Though..."

"What? Is my dress too short?" She fidgets with the bottom of it, then tugs it down.

"It would look better on my floor."

She narrows her eyes at me. "That's *not* going to happen."

"Yeah, I know," I mumble, undoing the top button of my shirt. It's suddenly getting stiflingly hot in here. "Dance?" I ask her, unable to resist the urge to have my hands on her. She seems nervous by the idea but offers me her hand. The minute my hand clasps around hers, something feels right again. Like that's how it's meant to be, I walk her a few steps to the makeshift dance floor and pull her in close. She smells so fucking divine it's taking everything in me to not lean down and taste her.

"Look, about our discussion earlier—" Her hands fall to my chest.

"Let me fucking kiss you," I blurt out, cutting her off.

"Soren, we agreed." She steps back, and I let her.

"*You* agreed. I agreed to nothing."

"I've decided to date again," she announces.

"Good. When should I pick you up?"

"I'm *not* dating you." She huffs in exasperation.

"Well, I guess all your other dates will have broken limbs and have to cancel until you're available for me."

"Gosh, you are so annoying." She groans and shakes her head. "Actually, I have a question for you, and it's been playing on my mind for a while."

"Shoot," I tell her.

"I want you to be truthful with me."

"Okay."

She comes so close I could lean down and kiss those succulent lips. And I really want to.

"You appeared every time I was using my vibrator." I remain perfectly still and silent. "How and why?"

"Magic." I wink, and her baby-blue eyes narrow at me.

"How?" she pushes.

Sighing, I admit, "I slipped a listening device into your purse."

She considers this for a moment, then says, "Thank you for being truthful."

"You're welcome," I reply.

With a final assessing look at me, she turns on her heel and sashays off, and I don't see her for the rest of the night.

And trust me, I look for her.

Maybe I am in *love* with her.

Why the fuck did I tell her about the listening device?

Goddammit! I should have lied.

THIRTY-NINE

CRESSIDA

A listening device?

Who the fuck plants a listening device on someone who isn't an enemy?

How the hell did he do that without me finding it?

As soon as I arrive home, I pull out my things, and sure enough, a small device drops to the floor. I pick it up, and sure enough, it's small and easy to blend in. *Asshole.*

What else did he hear? It's not like I talk to many people. And there hasn't been any indication or mention from him about anything else. He always seemed to show up when I was masturbating. And I still don't have my vibrator back, which pisses me off.

Unsure of what to do with the device, I consider

flushing it down the toilet. But for some reason, I slip it into my phone case and leave it there.

Maybe I like him listening.

Maybe I'll keep it going for a little while longer and play with him.

It's only fair, right?

He intruded into *my space*. Granted, I did the same to him first, but at least mine was for work.

After removing my clothes, I climb into the shower. The water beats down, hot enough to sting, but I welcome it. Maybe it can wash away the thoughts I can't seem to escape. As I wash myself, I think of *him*. I spoke to my sisters a lot about Soren. They never seemed to *stop* asking about him. And I get it. He's a well-known businessman, and he's one of the most eligible bachelors there is right now. And Izzy seems to think he only has eyes for me. I strongly disagree with her, but tonight at the party, I could feel his stare burning into my back for a good thirty minutes before I finally turned around. And when I saw him, it was confirmed that he was indeed watching me.

I never once thought this would be the outcome of my trying to do a story on him. He's attractive, sure. You would have to be blind not to see that, but he always seemed so out of reach, a world above mine. Yet, somehow, now he is attainable, and he keeps showing up in my life. Keeps on making my stupid heart flutter at the sight of him.

I hate it.

And I love it at the same time.

My love for Noah grew slowly, and he gave me time to fall for him.

With Soren, it feels like I'm crashing in waves, struggling to breathe, and can't get up. He keeps pushing me back under, at the same time giving me his breath to breathe.

It's fucked.

And I need to make it stop.

But even as I turn off the water, I can still feel him on my skin. It's like no amount of scrubbing could ever get him off me.

OLIVER HAS BEEN NAGGING me about training with Soren. Noah even brought it up, asking if he could attend one of the first training sessions. I never actually agreed to it, but when I saw Soren in the office yesterday, I asked him about it, and he told me to bring Oliver to the gym where he trains tonight.

Now standing outside, the air smells faintly of

sweat and disinfectant, with the thud of gloves against punching bags echoing softly through the walls. My stomach twists, and it's not from nerves, but from not knowing which version of Soren I might face tonight. The one who looks at me like I'm already his, or the one who pretends I don't exist.

Noah is already there, holding Oliver's hand, when I walk in. The gym looks quiet for a weeknight, the hum of fluorescent lights filling the silence between us. Oliver can't stop smiling as I walk up to them, his excitement radiating through the air. He is utterly unaware of the tension curling inside me.

"He's good for this?" Noah asks.

"He said so," I reply.

I didn't see Soren at work today, so I couldn't confirm with him. I've actually only seen him once this week, and I've heard it's normal for him to be out of the office often, as he runs multiple businesses.

Layla told me, and I quote, *"He hires reliable people like you to run the businesses, and he stops in periodically to check on things."* If he thinks I'm reliable, I guess I'll take it.

As soon as I look around, I see Soren in the middle of the ring. He's shirtless, with a pair of jeans hanging loosely on his waist. There is a man opposite him who is holding up pads as he punches them.

Oliver appears to be awestruck. His eyes are large and round, almost sparkling, as he stares at Soren in the ring. He's never found a sport he loves, but by the way he's watching Soren, I think it may actually be boxing.

"He's good, Cressida," Noah says, eyeing Soren. *Maybe he's a little in love with him too.* I giggle to myself internally at that thought.

The man in the ring with Soren notices us first, and he motions for Soren to stop. He says something to Soren, who then glances behind him to find us waiting. His gaze moves to Oliver, then Noah, before landing on me, where it stays.

"You came," he says.

I take Oliver's hand. "If you still have time and are willing, Oliver would love a few pointers." Soren turns back to the man assisting him and says something, and the man leaves the ring.

"Of course. Care to get up here with me, little man?" Oliver nods his head eagerly as he climbs into the ring. "We have to warm up first, okay? You should always make sure your muscles are ready for whatever you are about to do."

Oliver hangs on every single word Soren says to him.

Noah and I stand back as we watch them warm

up, then the man from earlier comes out with a pair of small boxing gloves and hands them to Oliver.

"Oliver likes him," Noah comments, and I nod. I know he does. The way he watches Soren and listens to him... He never listens to us that intently. With a glow in his eyes, as if he's eating up every single word. "And he certainly keeps you on your toes," he jokes.

I hear Soren tell him not to use any of these moves on anyone, and Oliver nods in agreement. We stay there for a good hour, until Oliver starts getting tired. Soren notices and pats him on the shoulder, telling him he did a good job. Oliver climbs down and immediately runs up to us. We tell him he did a fantastic job, and he thanks Soren again before Noah takes him home.

"Get up here," Soren says to me.

"Why would I do that?" I ask. Looking around, I notice there's no one else in the gym. "Why is it so empty?"

"Because I told everyone to leave."

"You have that power?"

"Yes, it's my gym." He holds out a hand to me, and I take it. Then he helps me climb between the ropes, and as soon as my heels hit the ring, he bends down and starts removing them. "Barefoot in my ring, please." I let him take them off, and he places them to the side.

"Spread your feet, dominant foot slightly back," he instructs, and I do as he says, even wearing a skirt, which he finds amusing. "Curl your fingers tightly into your palms, elbows tucked in." He touches my elbow. "Now, try to hit me."

I relax my hands and shake my head. "I'm not hitting you."

"Hurricane, you won't be able to land a blow, so throw those punches." And the cocky bastard winks.

Fuck it! I ball my hands into fists and swing at him. And just like he anticipated, I completely missed. A smile plays on his lips, and it makes me even madder. I've been in many fights, mainly with my sisters, but I've never gone toe-to-toe with someone who has actual boxing experience.

I adjust my stance, then indicate for him to come closer with a crook of my finger. He raises a brow, and at first, I don't think he'll do it. But as he steps closer to me, I keep my eyes trained on his, and I reach around his neck with one hand. He allows it because it means I'm pressing against his body. He thinks I'm going to kiss him, but that's not what I'm going to do at all. As my fingers skim the back of his neck, I punch him hard in his stomach with my other fist. He grunts loudly, then a slow and sinister smile curves at the edges of his lips.

And I know I made a mistake.

The blow probably didn't even affect him.

But then I remember how he was injured, and my hands fly to my mouth.

"I'm sorry! Shit, are you okay? I forgot about your injuries," I fret.

He grabs me around the waist, and I'm helpless to stop him as he lifts me and then lowers me to the floor so he's now hovering over me, his knees bracketing me in, but not touching, and yet I feel him everywhere.

"I'm fine."

"But your ribs," I say, and without thinking, my hands go to his ribs. He doesn't flinch at my touch.

His gray eyes seem to soak in all the features of my face, and the way he's looking at me makes me a little insecure. That is, until he cups my cheek, and I instantly feel something more than I should.

"I'll be fine," he assures me. "You're sneaky, though. Stabbing people, distracting them, and then using your powers." He winks.

"Whatever it takes to win," I say.

"Is that right?"

"Yup. Now let me up," I tell him.

"Now, why would I do a thing like that?"

"Because..."

"Because?" he questions, his attention locked on my lips.

I have nothing left to give.

His gaze won't stop flicking between my lips and eyes, as if he's asking for permission.

"Soren," someone says.

His body tenses. I feel it under my palm. He's on his feet in a flash, holding his hand out to help me up. I set my palm in his, and he pulls me up.

"I'm sorry. I didn't know," he says to me, then turns in the direction of the voice.

I peer around him at Maya, who is standing there. She usually has a judgmental expression when she sees Soren with me, but right now, she looks lost.

But I won't pity her.

No, she doesn't deserve that from me.

"Maya, what are you doing here?" he asks.

"It's been weeks, Soren. You have to forgive me," she pleads.

She appears quite pale, almost sickly, and her hair is greasy and lifeless around her face. She looks miserable.

"What you did was *unforgivable*," he tells her.

I glance at him and then back to her. She's crying now, and they seem to be real tears.

"I would never have hurt him. I only wanted you to remember how important family is. We are important to each other, as Cressida and her son. We have a bond."

He tenses at her words, but doesn't back down.

"We are not the same as them. I am not your father, Maya. I have helped you enough, and I can't keep doing it. It's unhealthy for both of us."

I see the tight line of his jaw, the way his hands clench at his sides. It's clear this isn't easy for him. Without thinking, I reach out, my hand brushing against his. He takes it without hesitation. In that simple touch, I feel the weight of what he's doing, drawing a line, protecting us both, even if it hurts him. For the first time, I understand just how much this means to him. And suddenly, my anger toward Maya fades, replaced with something softer, a quiet gratitude for the man standing firm beside me.

FORTY
SOREN

I ᴋɴᴏᴡ my sister well enough to tell if she's trying to pull one over on me. And right now, she definitely isn't. I know that she's broken, but I can't be the one to always put her back together. It's not my job anymore. She's a grown-ass adult, and she needs to start living like one. I've given her everything necessary for her to live the best life possible, and she keeps on blowing it.

I'm at the point that I have no idea what I'm supposed to do about it. So, I've thrown my hands up in the air and said, "Fuck it, she can work it out herself." I don't need to baby her, even if she is my baby sister. I got her this far, and I don't need to take her any farther. She's in her early thirties, and by now she should have at least a fraction of her life together, but she's barely held a job for longer than a few weeks. She likes to blame it on her sickness, but that doesn't prevent her from working. She uses it as a weapon, and I see that now. And I have to stop letting her do it.

Cressida's hand is in mine, grounding me in a way nothing else does. It's strange how something so small can settle all the noise in my head and give me clarity.

I don't *need* her.

I *want* her.

That's the difference.

Needing someone feels like weakness, and I've had enough of that in my life. But wanting her— that's deliberate, conscious. She is not my escape, but she is my calm. And hell, that might scare me more than anything else.

Maya notices. Of course she does. It's hard not to notice because I won't let Cressida's hand go, no matter what.

Her first mistake was offering it to me.

Now I have her trapped, never to escape.

"Soren, *please*," Maya whines.

"Keep working, show me you can change. But for now, you aren't my priority," I tell Maya.

"That does not mean you can take my son again.

I have nothing to do with any of this," Cressida inter-jects hotly. "Next time you do something so stupid, not even your brother will be able to stop me."

"I see it now, I do. And I'm sorry for doing that to you," Maya says to Cressida. "I hope one day you can forgive me. I never meant the kid any harm. I just didn't know how else to make my brother see that we are all each other has."

"But you aren't. Some people go their entire lives without family. Family is what you make it, so make your own and love your brother for everything he's done for you. Right now, you use him and abuse his generosity. Why? Because he has money? Because you are the only woman he struggles to say no to?"

I squeeze her hand. She's wrong about one thing —it's not my sister I struggle to deny. It's Hurricane, the black-haired raven next to me.

My sister's gaze slides to me.

"I've started therapy," she says. "With Arlo."

Why did he not tell me that? Granted, I've been avoiding a lot of things lately and not talking to many people. It's hard when you feel like your life is a fucking shithole.

"Good," I tell her.

She glances back at Cressida again. "I should go." Maya's voice is small and quiet.

"You should," I agree.

She gives a stiff nod, then turns and leaves. There is a part of me that wants to feel sorry for her, but I don't. My only concern right now is the woman whose hand is still in mine. I need to work out how I can keep her, how to make her mine.

"I should go too," Cressida says, and tries to pull her hand away, but I don't let it go. Instead, I tug her into my chest, our bodies pressing together, and slide my hand up to her cheek. I love touching her face. This woman expresses so many emotions every time I do it. Like right now, her blue eyes are locked on mine, wide with surprise.

If I cracked her head open, could I see what she's thinking?

Probably not.

And to be honest, her head is way too pretty for that anyway.

"Stay," I say.

"I can't."

"We need to talk about us," I tell her.

Her hands lift and cover mine, where they rest against her cheek. "We probably should," she agrees.

At least she isn't telling me no.

That's a start, I guess.

"I really want to kiss you right now," I admit.

"Maybe you should take me out for dinner first," she says, her perfect lips curving up into a smile.

"Dinner?" I ask, raising a brow. "That I can do. When are you free?"

"How about tomorrow night?" she asks.

"Done. I'll pick you up."

"We're not going to your house either. It needs to be somewhere public, so you can't have your way with me."

I stroke her cheek with my thumb. "But I like having my way with you."

"I know," she says, then steps from my arms.

Okay, no kissing tonight.

But tomorrow night, I plan to kiss every part of her.

If she allows me, that is.

FORTY-ONE

CRESSIDA

"So, are you officially seeing Soren now?" Noah asks as he waits for Oliver to run and grab his iPad.

I'm dressed and ready to head out for my date with Soren. When I spoke with him a little while ago, he said he'd be here in twenty minutes to pick me up. I was hoping Oliver and Noah would be gone before then.

"It's just a date," I tell him.

"Well, for what it's worth, I actually like him. Even if he has a crazy sister who should be locked up." He chuckles, I wrap my arm around him, and he hugs me back. "I would say I'd beat him up if he doesn't treat you right, but we both know I would lose."

I laugh as we end the hug, and when I look over

Noah's shoulder, Soren is standing there. He eyes Noah suspiciously but says nothing.

When Oliver turns the corner and sees Soren, he runs straight to him. He holds a fist out, and Soren bumps their knuckles together. I can't help the warmth that blooms in my chest at seeing them interact like this.

"Hey, little man. Where are you heading off to?" Soren asks Oliver.

"With Dad. Are you here to see Mom or me?" Oliver asks.

"You, of course. Just wanted to check in on how your practice is going," Soren replies, giving him his full attention.

"It's going good. But Mom yelled at me for practicing by hitting the wall." He shrugs his shoulders, and Soren shakes his head.

"No walls, just a punching bag or practice with me, okay?" Soren tells him.

Oliver doesn't waste a second as he turns to Noah and me and says, "Can we go to practice? I want to practice."

"Oliver, you know we're meeting Taylor for dinner," Noah reminds him. "Maybe another night."

"Let's make plans," Oliver says to Soren, his eyes lit with excitement.

"Okay, I'll schedule it with your mother," Soren agrees.

Noah rests a hand on Oliver's shoulder. "Come on, time to leave. Say goodbye."

Oliver gives us both a wave before he runs to Noah's car and climbs in, Noah trailing behind him.

"You're early," I say to Soren.

"And you look beautiful," he replies as he gives me a once-over. "Though I'm getting a little jealous of your dresses," he adds.

"What?" I ask, confused.

"Because the dress is lucky to be hugging you so tightly," he deadpans.

I throw my head back and laugh. "Who knew you were funny?"

"Funny? I was being serious." And I can see by his expression that he was.

"Well, I'm jealous sometimes too," I tell him as I grab my purse, then shut and lock the door.

I descend the three steps until I'm standing in front of him. He takes my hand, and to be honest, I expect nothing less.

"Pity I can't ravish you tonight," he says. "You know, because we'll be in public."

I laugh again, not able to help myself as he leads me to the car and opens the door for me. I climb in, and when I look up, I find his gaze locked on me. He winks before he shuts the door and goes around to the other side and gets in. His driver starts the car, and we take off down the street.

"Not driving tonight?"

"No, I thought tonight I would drink with you," he replies.

"You rarely drink." I note.

"I don't like my senses dulled or to have my inhibitions lowered."

"And you feel like you can do that with me?" I question.

"I can lower everything but my cock when I'm with you."

Another laugh bubbles out of me, and I reach over and grab his hand this time, instead of waiting for him to hold mine.

"Oliver likes you, and that means a lot. Because if he didn't—"

"I like him too. He's a good kid."

"Do you ever want kids?"

He cracks his neck before replying, "I feel like that question is a trap."

I shrug. "I want you to be honest with me."

"Okay." He squeezes my hand as the car slows down. "No, I don't want kids. I pretty much raised my sister when I was basically still a kid myself. And doing that again doesn't appeal to me." We sit there quietly until the car stops. His driver goes to open the door, but Soren holds up his hand, stopping him.

"How does that make you feel?" he asks hesitantly.

"Not everyone feels the need to be a parent, and that's okay," I tell him. "Oliver is all I want. I don't want more kids."

"Oliver is a good kid. I enjoy being around him." His words warm my heart.

"Oliver already has a father, and Noah is a great one."

He nods, seeming to be happy with that answer, then he gets out of the car. He holds the door open for me as I slide across the seat. Once I'm standing on the sidewalk, I notice we're outside again at one of the hardest restaurants to get a reservation, which I have been to before. It also happens to belong to his friend Arlo.

"And here I thought you were taking me back to a sex club." I laugh.

"If that's where you'd rather eat, we can go there. They don't serve food, but I can think of something for me to eat." He rakes his gaze over me, and I blush. I can't help it.

We enter the restaurant, and the hostess recognizes him immediately. She guides us to a more secluded area in the back, where a table is already set with a bottle of wine, two glasses, and menus. He pulls out my seat as the hostess excuses herself. When I sit, he leans down and kisses my neck softly before taking his own seat.

"I have a question," I say. He nods and then pours us each a glass of wine. "Would you take me to one of your girlfriend's parties?"

He adamantly shakes his head. "No, never."

"I've heard about them. People share. Would you not like to share me?"

"No, I wouldn't. I would take you to the wife one, though."

I grin, his answer pleasing me. "I'm not your wife," I point out.

"No, I guess you aren't... *yet.*"

I pause at the "yet," and I hold back from commenting, even though I know he's waiting for me to speak.

When he decides I'm not going to respond, he asks, "Would you like me to order for you?"

"Yes, I'll eat anything. I'm not fussy."

He orders each of us a steak and a dessert for

after. When the waiter walks away, Soren reaches across the table and takes my hand.

"I'm not going home with you tonight," I remind him.

"Yes, I know. Maybe tomorrow?" Soren asks, hopeful.

"Maybe," I reply.

And he smirks.

THE FOOD IS IMPRESSIVE, but I knew it would be. We have great conversations about various topics, and I'm surprised at how much I like listening to Soren talk. When he speaks to you, he gives you his full attention. It's special because not many people can talk to someone without their gaze flicking to something else.

He makes me nervous, but it's a good type of nervous. The kind that makes me wonder where this will actually go now that we're both open to it.

I'm glad our thoughts on having children are similar. I wouldn't want to be with someone and deny them a child if that's what they wanted, because it's a blessing to have a child, and a lot of people don't get that opportunity.

As we leave the restaurant, his hand isn't holding mine for a change. Instead, his arm is wrapped around my waist, and he keeps me close to him.

When we pull up outside my home, he gets out with me and walks me to my door. After I unlock the door, I turn to find him already stepping back, putting distance between us.

"What are you doing?" I ask.

"I won't kiss you or touch you until tomorrow," he says, and disappointment fills me, even though I am the one who put up that barrier.

"Thank you again for tonight. It was nice to see a new side of you."

"Anytime." He winks, and I go inside and shut the door. Leaning against it, I sigh.

Part of me wanted him to come in with me. Actually, no, all of me wanted that. I know we went too hot and heavy to begin with, but I have never felt this way for anyone before, not even Noah. And I married that man and had a baby with him.

Pushing away from the door, I hear a noise coming from the other side. Taking off my high heel, I raise it above my head, ready to use it as a weapon if necessary, just as the door opens. And standing there is Soren, with the key he stole from me.

"Do you plan to stab me with that?" he asks, a hint of amusement in his tone.

"Depends."

We stare at each other for a beat, then I drop the shoe and launch myself at him. He catches me and somehow kicks the door shut behind him as my legs wrap around his waist. Our lips smash together in a frantic kiss. His hands slide under my dress until they reach my ass.

He carries me down the hall, not stopping until he enters my bedroom. He gently places me on the bed, disconnecting us, and I instantly wish he hadn't. He starts to undo the buttons of his shirt, and I sit up on my knees so I can pull my dress off over my head. His gaze meets mine, and it's like he forgot what he was doing as he soaks me in.

"Are we going too fast?" I ask.

"Move in with me," he blurts, and I shake my head, taken aback.

"Now, that's *too* fast."

"I'll move in with you, then," he counters, and kicks off his shoes before he undoes his pants.

"*Soren*," I say in a scolding tone.

"Marry me."

I laugh at his outrageous requests until he's

standing in front of me naked. The sight of his nude body shuts me up quickly.

"I'll take you to the courthouse as soon as it opens if you say yes." And strangely enough, I believe him.

"We would need a prenup."

He smirks at that, as if he's just happy that I'm considering it.

But I'm really not.

Am I?

Why would I do that?

"I don't need one. You can have everything if you leave me." He steps toward the bed, eyes open and honest. "I only need you."

"How romantic," I gush as I lay a hand on his chest.

"I'm not romantic, and I'm not joking." He rests his hands on my hips, and I lean closer to him. He reaches behind my back and unclips my bra, then pulls it from my body. His finger lifts my chin to look at him.

"Marry me."

"Fuck me," I say back.

"That I can do."

His lips crash down on mine. His arms wrap around me, and then he proceeds to lay me back on the mattress. His mouth leaves mine, and he drags his teeth over my chin and down my neck until he reaches my nipple. He bites it, hard enough to leave marks, before he slides even farther down my body.

It doesn't take him long before he's at my vagina, spreading my legs wider to accommodate his broad shoulders. And then his mouth is on me. He does that thing with his tongue where he flicks it over my clit before circling it with the tip. It hits all the right spots, and it isn't long before I match his rhythm and press myself closer to his mouth. I can tell he likes it, because he lets out a growl and then repeats the process until I can't stand it.

My fingers clutch the bedding as I come hard. Soren's mouth disappears from between my legs, and a second later, I feel him at my entrance. He slides in, ever so slowly, knowing how big he is, and pauses.

"You take me so well," he praises as he watches his cock press farther inside me.

"Deeper," I whisper, liking how it feels.

He pushes in some more, and I feel so good, so full, wanting him to start moving.

When I think he's almost all the way in, he pauses and looks at me. "Deeper?"

I nod, and he thrusts the rest of the way in.

I watch as he holds his breath, squeezing his eyes closed.

"Move," I demand, and he does.

He starts to move, slow and steady, fucking me like I'm a good girl, but at the same time, he looks at me as if I'm his world.

I hope to one day be that for him.

"You were made for me," he rasps as he fucks me.

I nod my head, unable to actually speak. I'm getting close, and I can feel that he's almost there, too. He slows his thrusts, as if he's trying to drag out each one, and it's magnificent torture.

After we both come, he pulls out gently and then looks between my legs. "Are you sore?" he asks.

"No."

"Good. I want to go again."

FORTY-TWO

SOREN

She thinks I was joking about marrying her, but I wasn't.

I *love* her.

I never thought those words would enter my head about a woman, but I really fucking love her. I never wanted kids, but I meant it when I said Oliver is a good one, and I look forward to getting to know him better. However, if she ever changes her mind and decides she wants more children, I will have kids with her. That's how deep I'm in.

She's still snuggled in bed, sound asleep, as I get dressed. She doesn't open her eyes until I come back into the bedroom, holding a cup of coffee for her. She smiles, sits up, and then takes it from my hand.

I clear my throat, preparing to tell her things I've

never said to another woman. I'm entrusting her with information that could destroy many people, not just me.

"The Forsaken is made up of members who have some dark past they want hidden, or some darkness they want to explore and not get caught while doing it. That's why it was formed generations ago," I explain.

She doesn't interrupt or ask why I'm telling her this.

"We have members in various businesses, organizations, and civil service positions, but one thing we all have in common is that we have money and influence. Money is a powerful thing, and it grants us the ability to cover up many vices and misdeeds. Namely, the hunt."

My original plan was only to tell her enough to hopefully satisfy her curiosity. But for some reason, I don't want to hide things from her. I reach into my back pocket, pull out my phone, and bring up an article about the red-headed man we used as prey in the last hunt.

"You've heard of him?" I ask.

She takes my phone and looks at it, skimming the article.

"I wrote this article," she says. "The things I

found out about that man were terrible. He should be buried and never found again." She hands me back my phone, and I slip it back into my pocket.

"I want to start a life with you. And I know you value honesty. And I have been honest and truthful with you, to an extent." I pause.

"I want you to be my wife, Cressida. I want you to attend Forsaken events with me. I am their Lord, but I am not a lord without a lady by my side," I tell her.

"There are some things I can't tell you about the hunt, though."

"It's okay, Soren, I trust you. You don't have to tell me anything you don't want to or can't."

"But I want to tell you everything. I don't want you to hide things from me, and I don't want to hide things from you."

"I won't hide anything from you," she says, and I believe her.

"I killed that man in the hunt," I confess. "And it felt good."

She takes a moment to absorb that, then says, "You killed him?" She says the words as if she can't believe what she heard, as if repeating them back holds more meaning.

"You had an idea of what the hunt is, correct?" I say to her to pull her from her headspace.

"Well, yes. But for you to confirm it—" she says with wide eyes.

"Most of the people we hunt deserve it," I assure her. "People like him."

"And do you like it?" she asks.

"I do. And I will *never* stop."

"I would never ask you to stop, Soren. I understand who you are, at least a part of you. I get that you have a dark side because I've seen it in the ring. But if this is going to work between us, you are never, and I repeat *never*, to bring this around my son. Even if I love you, I will leave you."

"You love me?" I ask, surprised.

"Tell me you heard me." She gives me a severe look.

"I heard you, and I would never expose Oliver to any of this. One thing you should know is how well I can keep secrets. You've been trying for years to find them." I head to her closet, select a white dress, and place it on the bed.

"And to think, all I had to do was sleep with you in order for you to open up," she jokes, then her gaze falls to the dress. "What's that for?"

"Get dressed, Hurricane. The courthouse is open, and you and I are getting married."

"Soren, I can't." She shakes her head.

"You can. And in a few months, we'll have a bigger wedding, when your family accepts us."

"They already do," she says, setting her coffee down and then getting up from the bed.

"What do you mean?"

She grabs her phone, brings up her sister Izzy's contact, and then shows me her text messages.

Izzy: Did you fuck him yet?

Izzy: Come on, sis, bang that man.

Izzy: Have you said "I love you" yet? Because that man was hooked.

Izzy: I want all the details!

I read them with a smile, then look back at her.

"Your family likes me?"

"Hold up, big boy. You've only met one sister. You still have to meet the other and my parents."

"I will."

"I'm not moving in with you..." She pauses. "Yet."

"And marriage?" I ask eagerly.

"Maybe in a few months." Her arms wrap around my shoulders as she rises to her tiptoes and whispers into my ear, "I still have a few hours before I have to get Oliver. Should we take a shower?"

Who am I to say no to this beautiful woman, even if I couldn't get her to marry me today? You can bet your last fucking dollar that I'm going to be trying every single day until she says yes. Because one way or another, I plan to get a ring on that finger, no matter how hard she fights me.

Then she'll be *all fucking mine.*

FORTY-THREE

CRESSIDA

Two Months Later

I see Soren almost every day, but barely at work.

At work, I see him maybe once or twice a week. But he comes over in the afternoons and cooks dinner for us. And we spend most of our free time together.

Every single day, Oliver asks when Soren is coming over. He's really taken a liking to him, and Noah and I are both happy that he has.

Soren hasn't mentioned moving in together since that first time, but we spend every night together as it is anyway, so it's just a matter of making it official and working out what that looks like.

Oliver is running out the door to meet Noah as Soren walks in. "You off, buddy?" Soren asks him. It's funny and heartwarming to watch him interact with Oliver. Soren is so tall, even more so than Noah. But that doesn't intimidate Oliver at all. He loves it. He enjoys jumping up and smacking hands with him as he runs in the other direction.

Soren takes him to his gym, and they train together once a week, even though Oliver begs me to take him more often. I finally relented a month into our relationship and let him pick Oliver up from school, even though I was a bit hesitant because of what happened with Maya. But I trust him more than I trust most people now, especially when it comes to my son. And now Oliver expects it almost every day. The thing is, though, Soren is happy to do it. He tells me most of his work is done by noon. Plus, he's the fucking CEO, so he can do whatever the fuck he wants—his words, not mine. I always laugh when he says things like that because I know he's being truthful.

"You're ready?" he asks, eyeing my dress. It's blue to match my eyes. He told me his favorite color is the blue of my eyes, so I figured I would wear it for my first Forsaken event.

He's invited me to a few events, but I had to

decline because I had Oliver. He's come back after every one and climbed into my bed only a few hours after leaving. He never stays at the events for long anymore, and I wonder if I'm to blame for that or if his members already hate me. I also think about what type of person it makes me that I don't hate the idea of these hunts, with the Forsaken removing the scum of the earth. And I try not to dwell on that, and whatever it is he can't share with me about the hunts.

"I am, are you?" I ask. His suit, including the shirt, is black, but he has on a tie that matches my dress.

"I am."

I grab my purse and follow him out, our hands joined. Any chance this man can get to touch me, he takes. He guides me to the car, as if I don't know the way, and then pinches my ass as I'm getting in. When I'm seated, he slides in right next to me and rests his hand possessively on my thigh.

This event is the "wives only" event. I told him I shouldn't go. He told me he wasn't going without me. So here we are, at an event where only married couples are present.

Someone opens my door, and I climb out, Soren right behind me. He takes my hand in his before we head up the stairs to the entrance.

When we enter, the room is dimly lit by chandeliers hanging from the ceiling. I look around and notice most people are coupled up and standing in groups. A few are speaking to each other near the bar, and a couple of the wives are chatting in one of the sitting areas.

If you were to walk in here, you'd assume it's a regular event. I actually wonder if the wives know what these events are really about. Soren informed me that a few of the wives know some information, but most think it's like a social club. When he told me that, I laughed and said, "What, like a country club?"

I recognize some of the faces from my research, but a lot are new to me. All of them make sure they come up and greet Soren, and he introduces me to all of them. But I know I'm not going to remember their names.

He guides me toward the bar, and that's where I see two members I know and their wives. One of the couples is Arlo and Cora. Reon is with his wife, Lilith, who I've heard is as crazy as he is, if not more so, though I guess she did send me an invite to their anniversary party, and that was odd considering I didn't know either of them. They look like they all just walked off a Paris runway, but their expressions remain flat until we get closer.

When Cora sees me, she pulls me in for a hug. "Arlo told me you two were a thing," she gushes. I look at Arlo, who can't take his eyes off her. You can tell he loves her.

"Yeah, I guess we are," I reply.

"She's my soon-to-be wife," Soren interjects.

"Oh, you proposed?" Lilith asks, joining the conversation.

"No, he just keeps telling me that," I say, and he raises a brow at me.

"You will be."

"It's why you're here, Cressida," Arlo adds.

"How is Maya?" Soren asks Arlo, and several of us tense at her name.

"I heard you've been avoiding her," Arlo says.

"I have. It's best for the time being," Soren replies, voice both steady and sorrowful.

"I think you two should work out to what capacity you want Maya in your life," Arlo suggests.

Just then, Lilith hisses, "Why is she here?"

I turn my head to see Maya coming our way. She eyes us somewhat warily before she makes it to us and stops a few feet from Soren.

Reon and Lilith walk away, not wanting to be around her, while I stay still, glued to Soren.

"Soren. Cressida," she greets, nodding to us both but looking at her brother.

"I can go. Let you two talk," I offer.

"No, you are my family. You stay," Soren insists, and I see Maya visibly flinch at the words.

"I want to start anew. I've been working. Doing therapy. And I'm trying to change. Do you think you can accept me back?" she asks.

"It's not me you need to ask. It's not me whom you hurt so badly," Soren tells her.

Maya turns her attention to me now. "You are clearly someone special to Soren, and I accept that." I raise a brow at her. "I do. I've come to realize I can't continue to use him the way I have. I want to have a new and better relationship with him and with you, if you will let me. I won't come around unannounced, and I promise to keep my distance from your son."

I want to tell her to get fucked, that I would never allow someone so crazy in my son's life. Yet, as I look up at Soren, I want him to have a relationship with his sister because family is *important*. I understand that more than anyone. I love both of my sisters, and I know I would be lost without them. So, part of me can empathize with the loss she's feeling over not having someone who has always been hers.

"It will take time. A *lot* of time. But, yes, I will try," I finally tell her.

She nods and then excuses herself.

We're all quiet until she's out of earshot, and Arlo speaks, "Well, that was good work. You have a woman with her head clearly on right," he says.

"Yeah, now if I could just get her to marry me," Soren says, looking down at me with a half grin.

"Tomorrow, nine a.m. Meet me at the courthouse," I tell him.

Arlo looks on with amusement, and Cora beams at us.

"Done," Soren says, but then his usual calm cracks just a little. His eyes darken with something raw, relief, maybe even disbelief, and before I can blink, he leans down to kiss me, slow and sure, like he's making the moment real for himself.

Tomorrow, I will be his wife.

But tonight, I will be his Hurricane whore.

EPILOGUE
SOREN

THE COURTHOUSE ISN'T what most people imagine when they think of forever.

No flowers. No aisle. No white dress trailing across polished floors. Just the faint hum of fluorescent lights and the soft sound of papers being shuffled.

But when Cressida's hand slips into mine, the world stills.

Her thumb grazes the edge of my palm, a quiet reminder that somehow, against every odd, every obstacle, we have finally found our way here.

She's in a simple cream-colored dress that hugs her curves and makes my chest fucking ache. Her hair is down, loose, and defiant, like her. Arlo's leaning against the back wall, smirking like he planned the whole thing. Cora's wiping away tears she swears aren't falling, and Oliver is standing beside me, beaming like the sun.

When the clerk asks, *"Do you take this woman to be your wife?"* the word "Yes" comes out steady and easily.

No hesitation.

No doubt.

Just truth.

Cressida's eyes glisten when it's her turn. Her voice wavers only once, but I feel the strength behind every word.

When the officiant pronounces us husband and wife, I don't wait. I pull her in, hand on her jaw, mouth on hers, claiming her in front of everyone because subtlety was never my thing.

She laughs against my lips, that sound I never get tired of, and whispers, "You didn't even let me finish breathing."

"Get used to it," I murmur against her mouth. "You're stuck with me now."

Later, when the papers are signed and the small crowd thins, she looks at me over her shoulder with that teasing glint in her eyes. "Still want to boss me around, Mr. Husband?"

I grin, sliding my hand to her lower back. "No, Mrs. Husband. Tonight, I'm all yours."

And as we step out into the sunlight, her fingers tangled with mine, I realize something I never thought I'd admit...

I didn't just find peace.

I found home.

THE HOTEL ROOM smells faintly of champagne and Cressida's perfume—sweet, heady, and goddamn dangerous.

Cressida stands by the window, the city lights spilling across her skin. She's out of her courthouse dress now, wearing one of my shirts instead. It hangs loose on her, the sleeves swallowing her hands. She looks over her shoulder at me, and that smile hits me harder than anything else today.

"Married," she says, testing the word like it's foreign on her tongue.

"Yeah," I answer, my voice rougher than I intend. "Didn't think I'd *ever* be that guy."

"And yet..." She turns entirely, walking toward me, barefoot and unhurried. "Here you are."

When she stops in front of me, I reach for her

waist and pull her in. My ring catches against the hem of the shirt, a small metallic reminder that this isn't temporary.

Her fingers brush along my jaw, and the look in her eyes undoes me—equal parts love and challenge.

"You're quiet," she murmurs.

"I'm thinking."

"About what?"

"How I went from wanting to keep you out of my life to wanting to keep you in it forever."

Her laugh is soft. "Forever's a long time."

"Not long enough," I reply and mean it.

She leans in and, presses her lips to mine, slow and unhurried. The kind of kiss that doesn't demand, it promises a lifetime together.

When she pulls back, her forehead rests against mine. "You know," she whispers. "For someone who claims not to need anyone, you sure can't stop holding me."

I tighten my grip on her hips. "That's because you're *mine* now."

We end up on the bed, limbs tangled, laughter soft and real. There's no rush, no edge of uncertainty, just two people who have finally stopped running from what's been there all along.

Later, when she drifts off against my chest, I

stare at the ceiling, my hand tracing lazy circles along her back. The world outside keeps moving, but in this small, quiet space, everything feels still.

She's home.

My chaos.

My calm.

My wife.

My perfect Venomous Deceit

ALSO BY T.L. SMITH

Black (Black #1)

Red (Black #2)

White (Black #3)

Green (Black #4)

Kandiland

Pure Punishment (Standalone)

Antagonize Me (Standalone)

Degrade (Flawed #1)

Twisted (Flawed #2)

Distrust (Smirnov Bratva #1) FREE

Disbelief (Smirnov Bratva #2)

Defiance (Smirnov Bratva #3)

Dismissed (Smirnov Bratva #4)

Lovesick (Standalone)

Lotus (Standalone)

Savage Collision (A Savage Love Duet book 1)

Savage Reckoning (A Savage Love Duet book 2)

Buried in Lies

Distorted Love (Dark Intentions Duet 1)

Sinister Love (Dark Intentions Duet 2)

Cavalier (Crimson Elite #1)

Anguished (Crimson Elite #2)

Conceited (Crimson Elite #3)

Insolent (Crimson Elite #4)

Playette

Love Drunk

Hate Sober

Heartbreak Me (Duet #1)

Heartbreak You (Duet #2)

My Beautiful Poison

My Wicked Heart

My Cruel Lover

Chained Hands

Locked Hearts

Sinful Hands

Shackled Hearts

Reckless Hands

Arranged Hearts

Unlikely Queen

T.L. SMITH

USA Today Best Selling Author T.L. Smith loves to write her characters with flaws so beautiful and dark you can't turn away. Her books have been translated into several languages. If you don't catch up with her in her home state of Queensland, Australia you can usually find her travelling the world, either sitting on a beach in Bali or exploring Alcatraz in San Francisco or walking the streets of New York.

Connect with me tlsmithauthor.com